DEAD OCTOBER

DEAD OCTOBER

CASTLE CAGE

Dead October

Copyright © 2020 by Job Martinez. All rights reserved.

No part of this publication may be reproduced, stored in a retrieval system or transmitted in any way by any means, electronic, mechanical, photocopy, recording or otherwise without the prior permission of the author except as provided by USA copyright law.

The opinions expressed by the author are not necessarily those of URLink Print and Media.

1603 Capitol Ave., Suite 310 Cheyenne, Wyoming USA 82001
1-888-980-6523 | admin@urlinkpublishing.com

URLink Print and Media is committed to excellence in the publishing industry.

Book design copyright © 2020 by URLink Print and Media. All rights reserved.

Published in the United States of America

ISBN 978-1-64753-535-3 (Paperback)
ISBN 978-1-64753-516-2 (Digital)

17.09.20

DEAD OCTOBER is dedicated to Erik McAllister: the man who inspired me to be the best version of myself. Erik McAllister passed away August 3, 2019. He has left an imprint that can never be replaced. His life was taken too soon, but beforehand taught me everything I needed to grow in life; as he inspired me, I plan to inspire others.

Erik Anthony McAllister
(10/08/77 - 08/03/19)

CHAPTER 1

Randy and Nicole

I was dead asleep, curled up in my blankets. Shit, I was practically dead to the world. I don't really know how to explain it, but anyone who drinks knows the feeling of being in a deep, dark sleep and suddenly feeling the hangover crawl into you like a vicious monster. I could just feel the hangover creeping its way in; the tension in the back of my skull pulled me in and out of sleep. I looked at the clock next to the bed: 6:10 am. I still had some time to sleep a little before dawn broke fully. The glare of the sun shone through my curtains, illuminating my bedroom in its glow. It was thick and its glare scorched past my eyelids, past my eyeballs, burned the back of my brain and forced me to wrap the sheets around my face. The damn heat from the sun turned what was my normally cool, comfy bed to a hot sweaty sauna; making everything from my hangover infinitely worse. My thoughts were heavily focused on the tension growing at the base of my skull. 'THANK GOD it's quiet enough for me to sober up', I thought to myself, as I hoped everyone was still asleep. I don't think I'd be able to handle my loud ass damn kids right now. Just when I thought things were dead quiet and I was at the edge of sleep, a loud crash roared throughout the bedroom, jolting me so that I practically spazzed myself out of bed. 'Guess I was wrong. Maybe I'm not going to get to sleep in like I'd hoped.'

A sense of hopelessness came over me. I gasped for a deep breath, then mildly threw a temper tantrum, and quickly shut down once again. The blood from my entire body rushed to the top of my skull bringing with it a hint of dizziness. I tried to regain my consciousness and forced my eyes to focus, despite the yellow goopy crust that glued them shut. As I looked around the room everything seemed normal, including the sound of the clock next to the bed noticeably ticking. At that point I didn't give two shits about what was going on around me. Rolling over instantly turned what was a small amount of tension into searing pain which pulsated to my brain like a gunshot had blown off the top of my skull. The commotion from something heavy being slammed down came again, but this time it was repetitive. The commotion continued to echo throughout the entire house. My brain took in every screaming second of that God awful sound, which echoed like thunder rolling into the house. The crash was so loud that I could feel the vibration roll up the damn bed. I paused for a minute, waiting for something else to happen. The house grew suddenly silent, like time had stopped. I wasn't sure if it was all in my head, or if Evelyn, my wife, was bulldozing the house down. I couldn't stand to hold my head up any longer and flopped myself back against the pillow.

"What the hell was that?" I said in a frustrated tone as I pinched the top of my temples together, my eyes blurred and dry. The stenchy taste of alcohol baked at the back of my throat. The feeling was perpetual. I laid there knowing it wasn't a matter of *if* I was going to puke, but more a matter of *when*. I was that hungover. I prayed it wouldn't be a surprise puke session that would cause me to puke all over my own bed. I fought hard to hold it back; as best I could with my stomach wrenching and twisting. Vomit crept slowly up my throat. I swallowed it back down, forcing it down as my stomach pushed against me; a battle of which was the strongest muscle had commenced. Vomit twisted my stomach and I painted the bed sheets with last night's late drunken fridge raid.

Again, noises reached from down the hallway, but this time, it was a heavy scratching sound. Whatever caused that blasted sound had my attention, forced me to stare at the door confused; my brow squished. My heart jumped to the front of my chest; made each heartbeat feel like it was pulsating a million pounds of pressure to the top of my head. I was no longer dead to the world. I was an angry blob of flesh rolling around in bed. Damn it!

I mustered the energy to shout, "turn it down!", thinking the kids probably had the damn surround sound to the tv on high. My head still pounded from the long night of drinking whiskey with my good friend Mike McConnell at the tiny run down bar down the road.

The rustling continued, forcing me to shout out, or should I say babble out, "WHAT THE HELL IS GOING ON…..?". I waited for someone to answer my damn question, but the scratching sound came to a halt; no response.

"Evelyn…." I paused, waiting for someone to answer me. I was on the verge of completely losing my shit.

"Evelyn…." I yelled out, with a firmer voice this time, my patience was paper thin. I muttered a string of curse words, that I don't even think I really understood, and waited for my wife to pop her head into the room. Most of the time, Evelyn had some kind of damn project going where she was ripping a wall down or some other DIY shit.

"WHAT THE HELL…EVELYN?!" The lack of response from anyone in my household left me confused and angry. I flopped back and forth in bed, counting by seconds in my head, trying to calm my heart rate and regain full control of myself. Another wrenching twist in my stomach boiled up in my throat and caused me to burp up a little vomit; a tiny bit splashed the roof of my mouth. The taste of it lingered, no matter how hard I attempted to swallow it back down. I regurgitated and swallowed it again. The more I tried to keep it down, the more my stomach wanted to play tug of war. Just when I thought I was in the clear, vomit roared up my throat like a bullet, spraying out of my mouth into mid air and projected to the top of the ceiling before ping-ponging its way back down to my face. I tried placing my hand over my mouth to hold it in, cupped my hands, but it was too late. The shower of puke caught my face and pillow. The smell of it caused me to wrech violently, one more time ejecting the vomit, this time enough to flood my face and make me jump out of bed in shock.

Disgusted from bathing my face in my own fucking vomit, I grabbed a dirty shirt from the floor to wipe off. The room spun. I shoved my face back into the shirt, my back arched like a werewolf from fucking London. The vomit ricocheted off the t-shirt and splashed to my feet. I heaved once more and caught it into the shirt.

"Fuck...", I moaned, breathing in and out heavily. The pulse died down in my head and I instantly felt better. The mirror above my night stand showed my beard dripping with green chunks and...carrots? I didn't remember eating that at all. I was genuinely disgusted, deep down in my soul, but slightly cheerful at the thought of my battle wound vomit story. I couldn't wait to tell McConnell. I even managed a chuckle at the thought.

"Fuck me."

After the room came to a complete stop from my vomit tirade, I tip-toed over to my desk, almost slipped in my regurgitated mess I'd made...fucking weak. I had to use the wall to fully catch myself as my ankle slid across the wood floor and smacked on the corner of the bedpost. I reached for the towel on my desk chair. I pinched the towel with two fingers and pulled it to my feet to wipe the shit off my feet. The musk of the vomit made my stomach that much weaker. I tried to wipe my chest and beard to clear the evidence before Evelyn had a chance to see me. I glanced at my bed and realized it was soaked in vomit.

"Fuck, I'm just going to have to take the mattress out back and torch the fucker because that shit ass smell ain't ever gonna come out," I muttered angrily. The smell alone could make a fly puke...shit. I ripped the sheets off the bed and pinched the tip of my pillow trying to quickly roll it up into a ball. My foggy brain tried to think about how I could ninja my way out of the bedroom, down the hallway to the bathroom, and get cleaned up before Evelyn,or the kids, noticed me. Then again...I could just lay down again and go back to sleep. She was going to find out anyway so I might as well have felt better to receive the ass chewing of a lifetime that headed my way.

I was dead to the world once again. I grabbed her pillow and plopped my stank ass body back onto the bed. The cool pillow wrapped around my face as I paced my breathing and began to pass out. The pressure in my head throbbed slower and slower with each controlled breath. Another crash pierced through my attempt at peace from down the hallway and forced me to rise from my soft pillow; though I remained too paralyzed to actually get up. I popped my head up to stare at the door. God, I just wanted to ignore it; I didn't have a care in the world aside from rolling around the bed feeling man sick. Man Sick: when a male has a cold, headache, or is just plain fucking hungover, preventing this individual from doing anything. Even if the world was going to end, or if a nuke came down from the Heavens, this man would not, could not, move from his bed and his wife/girlfriend/caretaker would have to bring him every little thing he cried out for. Fuck, I probably deserved to suffer so much after last night. Punishment.

When it came to Mike, it was always a competition between the two of us on who could drink the most. The guy could drink like a fucking fish; any time, anywhere! Frat parties back in our prime had been epic because of this dude. Even just hanging out after work on a slow night; the dude never quit. I was always playing catch up with him when it came to the endless nights of drinking. Last night, particularly, though, I would say I was the whale of us both. I drank enough to fill all the mouths of a fucking college dorm. Once again I'd have to explain to Evelyn why I came home shit-faced drunk. I had my excuse all planned out: my tire went flat so I stopped to get a drink while I waited for the tow guy and I had to catch a cab home... but then again… I think I used that one before so maybe I didn't really have a plan. To be honest, I wished I could finally tell her the truth about everything and look her in the eye again.

Maybe it was just the fact that she and I had had one of the biggest arguments of our life together. How did I justify that I didn't even remember getting home? As some time passed, I laid there trying to get myself to go back to sleep, but my thoughts were moving like a freight train. I laid there trying to find a way to pull myself out of the dog house. It dawned on me that the house was way too quiet, now. That damn unbearable sunlight beamed like a laser on my face and baked the vomit I'd missed to my face and beard. A ringing echoed throughout the room which startled the shit out of me. My alarm was going off like a fire truck next to my ear; *beep, beep, beep*. I slammed my hand on top of the snooze button and missed the button entirely...beep, beep, beep. ripped the fucker from the wall, breaking the cord from the back end of it before chucking it at the wall behind me. With a new sense of calm, I fluffed my pillow and placed it softly next to me on the bed. My head was pounding with such intense pain it felt like it was going to last forever. My mouth was drier than a camel's ass. I tried my best to hold on to what was left in my stomach. I needed coffee and some aspirin; the quick fix for any long night of drinking.

"Shit." My wife was going to be so pissed.

"Evelyn..." I quietly muttered, in hopes that she would sympathize with me and come to aid my pathetic ass self. Yep. Man sick.

Half awake, I babbled her name, "Evelyn..."

I still hoped she would answer, but she did not come to love or rescue me. My worthless body was exhausted, weak; my eyes got heavy. Finally it was quiet enough to recover from this man sick disease that I brought upon myself and I drifted in and out of sleep.

2

When it came to my relationship with Evelyn, it always seemed like I couldn't do anything right. From the moment we met, we got off to a bad start, and yes, I would say it was always my fault. I'd either say or do something that perpetually dug me into a hole. But what I did that was causing me to drink myself to death was the worst of it all; the one thing that could never be forgiven. I knew that the moment I told her the truth, it would ruin our lives, our family, and our love for one another. What I did could never take away from how much I actually loved her. I wished there was some way to tell her why I'd been acting that way; to explain the constant drinking (I'd always been a drinker, but I'd been drinking more than ever) and the distance in our relationship, or why I couldn't even make love to her. The guilt and shame of it all ran through my mind like a bad movie. It was why I avoided her every opportunity I got, either hiding in the office, or coming home late, even when I didn't have to. Just the other night I'd gotten home late and she'd already been laying in bed. I'd just stood there, in the middle of the doorway, staring at her while she slept; completely unaware of my presence. The overbearing guilt that had been sitting in the middle of my chest ate at me. I'd just wanted to walk up to the bed beside her and tell her I loved her, that I needed her. I wanted to wrap my arms around her and kiss her; tell her I would do anything to take her away from harm. The thought of it sat at the back of my head as I stood in the doorway...my guilt sat heavily in the pit of my stomach. I knew that once I looked deep into her eyes, the moment our eyes connected, that I wouldn't be able to hold back and I would tell her about the affair I'd had with a woman named Olivia from work.

The light from the bathroom glared off her face as she laid there, so peacefully. I wiped my hands over my face hoping the shame would just fade away.

Fuck! I couldn't help myself, though. Olivia was this phenomenal woman, who had given me the slightest ounce of her affection and, like a schmuck, I had fallen for it. I had no excuse for what I did. I was a pig, scum of the earth, dog shit, if you will, scraped into a puddle of piss. This I knew, but just watching Olivia walk around in those tight dresses that hugged every inch of her body and showed off her long legs, was enough to pull me in. God, those smooth, big lips and beautiful blue eyes with thick brown hair all the way down to the small of her back, were mesmerizing. This woman would walk around the office and all the guys in the office wanted a piece of her. She had this look about her that had all guys trying so hard to take her home and fuck her as soon as any of them got a chance, but she didn't want those other guys - she wanted me - out of all people. I had nothing great to give her, but when we talked to each other, we had this connection I hadn't had with someone in a long time. She baited me. When I'd come to work angry and pissed about Evelyn, or something at home, she would be the one I bitched and complained to. She knew I was married, but still gave me every signal she could think of. She gave me her full attention...every ounce of her affection... baiting me like a venus fly trap. When I got vulnerable enough, she brought everything she had to the table. It was more than enough to push me into the category of dog shit. But God, the guilt ate me alive and I knew there was no coming back from any of it. Everything was changed forever. Evelyn would never look at me the same as she once did.

Olivia had stayed late at the office one night to help me finish filing papers from accounting. I was weeks behind and after a couple hours of innocent flirting and me bitching about Evelyn and I's relationship, Olivia finally said, " Can I be honest? I'm tired of hearing about your wife. What about us? I know you feel it too... just like I do."

I looked at her like it was a joke, but she wasn't kidding. She grabbed my arm and pulled me close to her body, forcing my hands to grab her tight ass, and looked me deep in the eyes; both of us dead quiet before she leaned in to kiss me. She waited for some type of resistance, but I'd wanted it just as badly as she had. After our passionate kiss, all she had to do was bite her lip and say, "Randy, you can have me any way you want me... just *fuck* me." I looked at her, scared, knowing it was the wrong thing to do, but thinking to myself: 'You're already this far...you already crossed the line anyway'.

    I had grabbed her as hard as I could and forced her body against mine; both of our breathing intensified. It was the all around sexiest moment of my life. My heart raced and my palms became waterfalls. Deep in my chest, I knew it was wrong, but the more the thought processed at the back of my head, the more I ignored it. I'd fallen into her arms, as she had into mine; both of us knew it was wrong, but were completely unable to deny each other. When I had seen her half naked, with her button up top taken down to her laced bra, I'd lost my mind. Both of us lost clothing standing there in my office. Olivia stood in a lacey thong and smoothly slid her hands all over my body. As my name softly slid out of her mouth, she bit her lip and threw herself at me. At that moment I felt special...more special than I'd felt in a long time. Evelyn and I had been married for almost 15 years and the romance had definitely died...a lot. In all honesty, it was never that passionate between us. It was something that had lacked in my marriage for a really long time. God, I wished there was some way to tell her, but like I said, things would never have been the same, so I did my best to keep it a secret. I knew it was a mistake that couldn't be taken back and was completely unforgivable; a mistake that would forever hurt her and the kids. It would have destroyed my family and I couldn't lose my kids and my wife. Regret had washed over me instantly after that first time, but being with Olivia was like taking a drug - the rush and adrenaline of it all got my heart pumping. The heat between our bodies...the fusion...was more than enough to have me coming back for more. And I went through with it every time, knowing how wrong it was. Worst of all...the more we did it, the more our passion grew. The drug got deeper and stronger into my soul, my body, my mind...I knew the destruction it would cause in my family, but I craved it, selfishly doing it anyway.

3

The house was quiet, my hangover was fading away, but the alcohol lingered in my system, powerfully. My eyes popped wide open as I noticed the house was a little too quiet for any typical weekday morning. Usually my daughter and son were screaming their heads off, fighting with each other. My oldest, Nicole, was always waking me up yelling about how her life was so unfair and no one understood her, or bitching about how Joey had done this or that. I forced myself to climb out of bed, gently brushed the crusted throw up off my beard and chest, and walked over to the closet to grab a t-shirt and some socks from the dresser. As I walked to the door, I slid my socks on, my legs felt too heavy to lift. My feet dragged across the wood floors in the bedroom as I rubbed my temples; my head still throbbed, my hangover still lingered (though slightly less than earlier). I slowly opened the door, using a soft voice, "Evelyn".

I stood in the doorway waiting for her to answer. "Evelyn?"

No answer, but a faint rustle came from down the hallway. I tried to bring myself to call out again without throwing up, "Evelyn?"

Again, no answer. I tried to come up with the strength to walk down to Joey's room to check on what the hell was going on. I walked, maybe stumbled, down the hall sliding my hand across the wall to keep myself from falling over in my dizziness. I paused for a moment, placed both hands on the wall, took a deep breath, then leaned on the wall next to my son's door. A soft rustle came from behind the door. I figured that Joey was getting dressed, so I waited and knocked, "Joey?"

I waited for Joey to answer; knocked once again. "Joey, do you know where your mom went?"

Still no answer. The rustling behind the door sounded like it was shifting back and forth. Something slid across the floor. With a firmer voice, I questioned, "Joey what the hell are you doing? If your mom's not here, get ready so I can take you guys to school!" My patience grew thin and I pounded my fist against the door.

A big bang came from behind the door, caught me off guard, jolted me. It forced me to jump back and I slammed my back against the wall. Confused and startled, I managed to utter, "Joey..."

The rustling behind the door came to a complete stop and at the bottom of the door a shadow paced back and forth, then came to a complete stop. With my back still against the wall, I stood there completely bewildered. Another loud ass bang startled me back from my confusion. The shadow under the door moved again. I had lost my patience. My voice was aggressive as I shouted out, "Joey!?"

No fucking answer. The shadow under the door stopped again. I held back vomit, with all I had, and reached for the door knob; grabbed it tightly and attempted to twist it. Locked. What the fuck? The rustling behind the door grew louder; finally from behind the door: BANG, BANG, BANG! The door punched outward towards me which caused me to jump back against the wall again. The frame of the door held the door back and it pissed me off. I lunged towards the door, grabbed the doorknob as tightly as I could, twisted it back. I thought maybe I could just break the damn knob off, so I squeezed tighter and tighter.

Once again I resorted to pounding my fist on the door, "Joey answer the damn door!" My weight pushed against the door as I prepared to slam my shoulder into it. Just before I swung my body into the door- BOOM- the sound of something large smashed into the back of the door. I was jolted to the wall once more, lost and feeling slightly afraid. I rushed from the wall back to my room. I figured that Evelyn probably had a pin to pop the lock hidden in her night stand. My shuffle through her nightstand had paid off. I located a safety pin and rushed back down the hallway; looked at the door cautiously. I stared at the bottom of the door for the shadow, but it wasn't there anymore. The light from the sun beamed from under the door. I gripped the doorknob and forced the pin into the lock hole and quickly heard the click of the lock releasing.

4

Gently and cautiously I opened the door. As I twisted the knob, my thoughts wandered. I figured that Joey was probably playing some type of damn game. I opened the door slowly…"Joey what the hell….." But there it was. I paused in shock. My eyes tried to process what I was looking at. I stood in the doorway of Joey's room stunned and horrified. Everything I had felt earlier: my hangover, anger, confusion… all of it was flushed away. I felt the blood in my skin drain away instantly. I had to have been pale as fuck. Every thought I had was dismantled and unprepared for what my eyes and mind were trying to process. A trail of blood led behind my son's bed. I found my wife crouched behind the bed, too. As I cautiously walked into the room, my socks soaked up the blood on the floor. My feet slid across the wooden floor in the pool of blood that flooded around the bed. I looked down and watched my socks soak up the liquid, in complete awe. The sunlight crept from the top of the blinds in the window and glared into my disbelieving eyes for a moment. I timidly walked around the bed, blinded by the light for a split second. Evelyn hissed as she huddled over something in the corner. I was completely terrified. I could barely speak, "Evelyn"…I paused for a second, waiting for any type of response from her. My heart jumped to the top of my throat and I felt faint as I moved closer to her.

"What the fuck are you doing, Evelyn?"

I heard crunching and snarling; the sound of bone and cartilage… bones twisted and popped. I was utterly terrified and stunned at what I was witnessing. Evelyn was crouched beside the bed, her back faced towards me. Her back arched so awkwardly. I moved further into the room, the sunlight moved past my eyes. The spots dissipated and I regained my focus. I brought both of my hands up to rub my face to stop my eyes from playing tricks on me. I leaned over to look at Evelyn's face and see what the fuck she was doing.

I asked again, "Evelyn? Babe, what are you doing?".

I froze, taking a deep breath, and stumbled back in utter shock and disbelief. It couldn't be true; no way could I have been standing there, actually witnessing that horrific scene. The trail of blood around the bed led to a bloodbath in the corner. Evelyn was crouched over my son's lifeless body. Her hands dug deep into his gut, pulling out anything she could get her hands on. She clawed and gnashed at him. Watching her caused my throat to close. Horrified, I placed one hand over my mouth and began to babble and mutter words...none of it made any sense. Evelyn continued to eat away at Joey's lifeless body. His eyes were wide open. It almost seemed as though he was staring at me dead in the eyes. I stifled a sob. No movement came from his face, except when Evelyn tugged something from his body causing his eyes and mouth to twitch open. My God! My wife was pulling apart our son with the hunger of a ravenous wolf obliterating its prey. Her head twisted and her neck cracked back and forth. She seemed completely unaware of my presence; lost in her massacre. I just stood there, trying to compute and understand what I was actually looking at.

"Evelyn..." I attempted to mutter to get her attention, unable to bear what she was doing to my boy. My jaw clenched tightly with paralyzing, intense fear. My pale lips shook. My entire body trembled, in fact. My wife...was...eating our son; she was fucking *eating* him, and I had no idea what to do. I wanted to pull her off and stop her; scream at her. I didn't know what to do. Evelyn was demolishing our son. I reached over to her shoulder, my hand shook so badly. Fuck, I was a pussy; so much for being my family's 'protector'. I touched her right shoulder and gently pulled her back. When I finally captured her attention, her head snapped back and the bones in her neck popped and cracked, disjointing themselves like something out of the exorcist movies. Her eyes: blood infused. She screamed at me at the top of her lungs with blood dripping from her chin and her mouth, splashing my arm with my son's blood. Her rapid movement caused her blood soaked hair to whip blood into my face as she snapped back and screamed again.

The warmth of Joey's blood slopped on my face and told me that Joey was alive just moments before I'd entered the room. Evelyn's once whitened teeth were stained with blood, like a newborn eating pasta sauce. She growled at me; a sound like I'd never heard before... an evil sound...a beastly sound. Petrified, I shakily wiped the blood from my face, shrouded by the fear of what was going to happen next. The blood in my eyes blinded me. Quickly, I tried to regain my vision by using my t-shirt sleeve to clean the blood from my eyes. Evelyn's entire body was covered in my son's blood and in both hands she held bits and pieces of him. She squeezed so tightly... mushing my son's insides through her fingers. Again, I attempted to get any type of human response from her.

Shaking with extreme fear and confusion I managed to mutter, "Evelyn...what the fuck did you do?"

I hoped to get a response from her; prayed that this was some type of cruel joke or pay back for the horrible husband I'd been. Hoped it was anything but what it seemed. My voice shook and I blinked fiercely as the blood caked to my eyelids. My throat closed so tightly it took a second for me to swallow the dryness in my mouth. I licked my lips and could taste the splatter of blood on the tip of my tongue. I backed away from Evelyn cautiously. She quickly leapt to her feet, her body twisted. I'd never seen her move so fast. Like the terminator, she scouted her attack, and lunged at me while screaming at the top of her lungs. Her arms and fists swung at me, in full rage, attempting to do any type of damage. She clawed at me as I fell back into my son's desk. My head crashed into the wall, almost busting a hole, I hit so hard. Her body smashed me into the desk again. She felt heavier and stronger as she pounded her body against mine and pinned me down. My foot slipped on the gruesome amount of blood on the floor as I tried to gain any type of leverage. Her hands swung at me, hitting me as hard as she could. I took numerous blows from her tiny fists, each one pounding viciously into my head and face. I never knew she was able to hit this hard. I attempted to grab hold of her while her teeth chomped at me. What the fuck was happening?

Her lip rolled up her teeth, washed over with blood, and she lunged at my chest. Her loose, twisted head flung at me and her teeth caught a small part of my t-shirt, pulling it away and ripping a section. I plunged the palm of my hand under her chin and pinned my hand into her throat. I could practically feel her spin at my fingertips. The more she resisted, the more I weakened. The tighter I squeezed at her throat, the less it seemed to affect her. Finally, I got a hold of one of her fists while the other still punched me. Both of us struggled in the fight. I held her back with all my strength; her body pinned me against the wall and desk. She snapped her teeth at me, growling. Suddenly, she paused. She was holding back; her lip quivered. Her blood infused eyes stared at me for a split second with her lip still quivering. Her entire body spasmed. One by one the muscles in her body flared and popped, forcing her entire body to convulse. For a moment I thought that my wife was finally coming back to sanity; our eyes locked and it was as if things were beginning to slow down. Time stopped for that moment, but I quickly understood that this was no longer my wife. I looked deeply into her once beautiful green eyes. They were now completely infused with blood. All that was left were two little black holes washed over with blood. For that split second though, things were calm. Then, just like a jet engine, the animal in her arose quickly and ten times more powerfully, pounding me against the wall pinning me. Evelyn came at me from all directions...faster, stronger, and more furiously than before. Her body pounded against mine, softening me, then jumping on top of me. Her tiny fists felt like boulders smashing against my face. She continued to scream in rage; a rage I'd never seen coming from Evelyn. While she scratched at me, she spat blood onto my face. Her jaw chomped back and forth and her tongue caught between her rapid jaw, snapping. Her anger rose.

Unaware that she was clenching down on her tongue with such force, she started to make it separate from her mouth. As she bit down with more rage, her tongue hung off and a piece of flesh showered me in blood. The loose blood vessels in her tongue sprayed blood with each heartbeat. Losing her tongue didn't even phase her. She reached over and pulled what was left from the small bit holding it together, ripping it off, unphased, slapping it to the ground. A mixture of blood and saliva dripped from her mouth. How was it possible for my wife to have that extreme strength? More and more blood loss consumed the both of us, making the fight harder to control. She had me pinned on top of the desk. Using the blood spatter as leverage, I rolled my body off the desk with all my force. I plunged one hand in her face and the other into her armpit. With all my might I pushed her away just enough to lunge my knee into her chest, creating the space to thrust her as hard as I could. She flew into the corner, her head hitting the side of my son's bedpost. She tripped over my son's lifeless body. She fell into the corner of the room smashing into my son's nightstand; my son laid there...lifeless. I glanced at him; still in pure shock and got up from the desk as quickly as possible. Fuck, I was tired. I wiped the blood from my face with both hands. Terrified from what had just happened, I shook uncontrollably. My mind couldn't process what had just happened. My wife slowly crawled to her feet, still screaming like a wild beast. For a split second, our eyes connected again, but this was not the same moment as before...it was a stare down. It was her calculating her next move. It was me calculating my next move. It was a standoff on who would draw. Her eyes so blood infused that it poured from them like tears. I picked myself up off the desk and gently placed my feet down to the floor. I noticed her tongue under my foot. Any sudden movement would force her to come after me again.

    I glanced at the door, told myself to run, but I remained struck with fear...unable to move, unable to speak. It felt like forever as I mustered up the strength and courage to escape. With all my power, without hesitation, I pushed my body off the desk. I sprinted for the door as hard as I could. My body slammed into the door with such force that it swung open, slamming against the hallway wall. Instantly, I knew she was right behind me. My body told me something was behind me, just like in a horrifying dream. My wife lunged at me; hurled herself over my son's bed in a matter of seconds. The door swung back into the small of my back as I turned to look over my shoulder. The knob plunged its way into my kidney. My wife stretched out her arm, grabbed the back of my shirt and pulled me back into the door. Her blood covered hands ripped easily. I attempted to pull myself away and hit the door which swung open like a brick wall and stopped her in her tracks. The shock of the door stopped her, but her grasp of my shirt didn't budge. Luckily, I was able to pull away in that split second, as hard as I could. I ran down the hallway and slid across the damn wood floors; fuck it was a bloody mix. Damn wood floors! It was like I was trying to run on fucking ice. The floors still had the swipe 'n shine that I'd buffed into the floor the previous weekend. I had to get away. I slipped and slid on the floor so badly that I had to use the hallway walls to stay upright. The door behind me swung open and Evelyn quickly rushed down the hall. She chased after me, only a foot or so behind me as we entered the living room. Her outstretched arm grabbed a chunk of my hair ripping my head back. With a blood curdling scream she lunged at me. My foot got caught underneath the sofa tripping us both.

    Both our bodies crashed into the coffee table and crushed it into pieces. The pain of my body slamming into the coffee table shot through my back. I couldn't help but to scream in pain from the piece of wood that stuck out of my side. It dug unforgivingly into my ribs, while my wife continued reaching for me with outrageous fury. She shrieked and climbed her way on top of me...straddling me. Both of us fought for leverage against one another.

5

Her tiny, yet powerful body pinned me down. Her strength over powered mine! Evelyn forced her way on top of me, spitting blood and not noticing that the end of the table leg penetrated through the small of her back. The leg was so far in. No one could have survived that. The table leg had completely impaled her; protruding through her stomach. She was unphased. It was as if it never happened. She made no acknowledgement of its existence. Nothing was in her way. Nothing stopped her from biting chunks of flesh from my body. Her jaw chomped back and forth violently. She gurgled; choked on her own blood and hissed through her teeth as she spewed blood at me. It took all of my might to fight her off. I gave just enough fight to hold her back. My hands slipped from the blood and I realized that I was screaming for someone...anyone...to help me! My heart knew that at any second I was ready to give in. I was weak and exhausted from fighting. She had unlimited strength!

Suddenly, my daughter swung the door open from her bedroom down the hallway, "Mom! What the hell?! Oh My God...MOM!!!!!!"

No...No....please don't come out here, I said in my own mind as Nicole walked past Joey's bedroom and noticed the trail of blood coming from out of his bedroom. Please go back, I begged internally. She noticed her brother's feet sticking out from the bottom of his bed. She fell backwards into the wall from the shock and panic set in. I could hear her screams of horror; afraid to even take one step further out of the hallway.

Her eyes scanned around in shock. The horror of what was happening washed over her, hitting her like a ton of bricks. The hallway was covered in blood. I could see the fear from the horror scene before her wash over as she walked past the trail of blood while her mother and I fought each other in the living room. Nicole screamed from the hallway, which caught my attention: and I had been screaming at the top of my lungs for *her*. "Nicole help! Fucking help me!" She cautiously walked down; frozen in fear.

Unable to process anything, she stuttered, "Wwe What....the hell is going.... on?!" Nicole struggled with her words.

"DAD! DADDY YYY!!" "MOOOOOOM!" Her face contorted in anguish as she looked at what used to be a normal life turned nightmare. Evelyn and I continued to struggle against one another. Evelyn attacked me; clawed and scratched; screamed furiously as I strained to fight her off.

I yelled, "Sweetheart, run and get help! RUN!"

Nicole stood there in pure shock and muttered, "Dad, what's going on?!"

I screamed as hard as I could, "RUN, NICOLE, AND GET HELP DAMMIT! GOOOOO!". The piece of wood pushed further into my side and stole my breath. Evelyn's strength grew and mine weakened. I slowly lost my breath. I could feel the wood tear further into my skin and muscle; it was through my ribs. The more Evelyn and I struggled, the deeper the wood thrusted into me...I couldn't keep going! Nicole charged at Evelyn and grabbed her shoulders. Evelyn's head snapped back towards our daughter, her neck popped and crackled. Evelyn grabbed Nicole's arm. She pulled her wrist towards her and attempted to take a chunk of flesh out of it. Nicole used every ounce of adrenaline that coursed through her veins and freed her arm from Evelyn's slippery, bloody grip.

Nicole screamed in horror, "MOM WHAT THE HELL ARE YOU DOING?!" That was my chance. I was loose from Evelyn's grip and her attention was fixated on Nicole. I thrusted my body into my wife, forcing her to lose her balance on top of me. In a panic, Nicole kicked her mom in the chest. Evelyn's body was thrown from the force onto the couch. Evelyn fell backwards; stumbled. The wooden leg from the coffee table stuck straight through her torso. The spray of blood seeped from the inside of her night gown. Nicole realized that her mother had the wooden leg from the table sticking out of her side and finally lost her shit. She screamed at the top of her lungs; a blood curdling scream that could be heard from miles away.

Without hesitation, or any remorse, Evelyn jumped up quickly and lunged after an unsuspecting Nicole.

I reached my arm around to my side and attempted to rise from the floor. My fingers gently touched the sharp shard of wood sticking out of my side. Evelyn and my daughter wrestled their way to the ground. My wife threw up blood like her insides were liquified. Chunks of curdled blood, blackish-red, oozed over my daughter's face. My wife snarled and hissed through her teeth. Nicole was doing everything she could to survive. She was pushing Evelyn away, shrieking in terror. I used the couch as a crutch, grabbed another broken table leg and painfully hurled myself up. With the biggest swing I could endure, I brought the corner of the leg crashing into Evelyn's skull. CRACK! The cap of her head popped off and her lifeless body rolled over as Nicole pushed her off.

She screamed, "DAD!" as panic overwhelmed her. She was hysterically crying and was just as strongly confused. Her hands rattled, frantically wiping the blood from her face. I walked over to her as pain shot through my ribs. I dropped the wooden leg to the floor to embrace her and calm her down. I desperately tried to collect my thoughts, and just held her as she frantically screamed, "DAD! WHAT'S WRONG WITH MOM?!" Nicole became more hysterical as we held each other in the hallway. Her mother lied there, lifeless, covered in Joey's blood. I couldn't help the tears that streamed down my own face. I killed my wife...I killed my wife...but my son, oh God! I sobbed. Evelyn viciously tried to kill us all. Silence filled the house when suddenly the house shook as if an earthquake had just hit. The drywall cracked like glass. Pieces of the ceiling fell on top of my daughter and I. I looked up through the hallway and saw that the door leading to the garage was violently flying off the hinges. A burst of fire blazed out of the door and all of the windows in the house blew inward. Fire erupted through the living room. The heat was so intense...

6

The fire torched the drywall and the house crumbled around us. It felt as if a tornado landed on top of the house. Fuck! The fire blew debris everywhere! My daughter screamed in terror as I held her tightly. I didn't know what was going to happen, or what to expect next. The house shook so violently that it brought all the pictures of my family... my...family...and the walls, crumbling down. I'd never been as terrified. All I could think as I held my daughter was, 'This is the end. This is where we die.' She hadn't stopped screaming and all I could do was attempt to protect her from the falling ceiling and pieces of wood. The unbearable booms pierced our ears; the violent vibration all around us engulfed the house. The floor shook violently, destroying the foundation. The floor before us fell into the basement. Everything was happening so quickly, I couldn't think straight. I wrapped my arms around Nicole and I lifted her with everything I had left. Both of us stumbled to the back of the hallway. I shoved her into the bathroom. I knew that it was just a matter of seconds before the entire house crumbled into pieces. I grabbed both of Nicole's arms and pushed her into the bathtub, then tossed my body on top of her. I could hear the breath in her plunged out as my body pounced on top of her. I desperately tried to cover her as fire and debris came bursting through the bathroom window. A sound I had never heard before engulfed us; a howling, ear piercing sound of crushing metal. Nicole frantically screamed as she caught breath.

"Dad, can you tell me what's going on?".

I could barely hear her. I think she was so scared that those were the only words she could muster. She kept repeating herself over and over. All I could do was lay on top of her and pray for it to be over. But each second that ticked by felt like eternity. I was just as scared, just as helpless, as her.

Somehow, the madness around us vanished. I opened my eyes, which I realized had been squeezed too tightly; my hands were wrapped around Nicole's head.

CASTLE CAGE

7

A horn blared from an alarm sounding off in the distance, blood curdling screams of chaos seemed to echo from everywhere. One final boom blasted off in the distance, shaking the house again. The ceiling of the bathroom moaned and the boards in the floor were ready to give way. The floor from the upper bedroom collapsed inward. I forced myself to take a deep breath, flinching, ready for anything to land on top of us. I exhaled...maybe for the first time since I'd woken up. My breath slowly released all my muscles from the tension. I tried to collect my thoughts. Nicole whimpered in fear.

"I think it's over sweetheart," I whispered reassuringly, but unknowing myself, if everything was going to actually be ok. "I think it's over." I peeked over the top of the tub to look around and ensure everything was safe.

I was hurt and exhausted, but I tried to hoist myself up from the inside of the tub. Nicole finally lost her patience and pushed me off of her, freaking out. She screamed in a frantic, panicked sobbing. Honestly, a thickening amount of shame washed over me; sense of failure; a sense of dread. My brain tried to process everything. Just 20 minutes before I'd been puking my guts out, afraid my wife was going to flip out about my drinking or find out about my affair, but she'd nothing like I expected. My son was murdered...by his own mom. The words 'he's dead' repeated in my head over and over. My hand nursed the wound on my side. Time just stopped. My ears were deaf and I sat back in the tub as I watched Nicole scream. She shoved me to the back of the tub. Her words hollow, soundless. The word _dead_ drowned everything out as it consumed my mind. A sense of relaxation came over me like my body had released all of its endorphins at once. A sense of ecstasy like a rapid rush of water splashed me in the face. Nicole cut through my calm as she screamed at me to tell her what the hell was going on. I got up, but an extremely sharp pain shot through my back and dropped me to my knees. I reached my hand around to see if I could pull the piece of wood from my ribs. I endured the pain as best as I could and reached over. With two fingers I pinched the piece of wood and gently pulled. A painful shock shot all over my body, took my breath away and crippled all my muscles. The warmth of my blood ran down my side. I reached for her, but she swatted my hand away.

"Get the fuck away from me!" I hesitantly held my arm out to her without wavering.

"Calm down. I know just as much as you do." Nicole looked right through me, lost in thought.

"WHAT THE FUCK HAPPENED TO MOM!?!" "WHAT THE FUCK WAS WRONG WITH HER?" Nicole screamed at me.

The look in her eyes showed that she'd placed all the blame on me. As I nursed my side with one arm, I reached the other out to Nicole to comfort her. Nicole slapped my hand away again.

"I need you to calm down, Nicole, or I can't do anything to help!" Nicole calmed her breathing slowly. My hand stayed extended. "I'm just as scared and confused as you are, but you need to calm down."

Finally Nicole released her guard and jumped into my arms as both of us sobbed hysterically. The house creaked around us, sounding as if it was moments from collapsing on top of us

"Come on sweetheart we have to go." I tried to think of any way to reassure her that everything would be okay once we got out of the house. "Let's go! We have to go. Get up. We can't stay here." I grabbed her wrist, forcing her to get out of the bathtub. My wound hurt so badly that it crippled me to my knees again. I stumbled up and opened what was left of the bathroom door, pushing debris away to clear a path. The door opened to reveal that our house had collapsed all around us. I could see my office relocated to the hallway from the upstairs; right where we were sitting moments before we'd run into the bathroom. I couldn't swallow; my mouth was drier than ever. If we wouldn't have moved we would have been crushed. I wondered if we could even get through the mess.

"Are we stuck dad?" Nicole said, as I looked at her processing and calculating what our next move would be. "What are we going to do dad?" Nicole searched for answers in my face. "Dad!" I was lost in thought. "DAD!"

I stood there thinking. I searched desperately for any option for escape. As I turned around I noticed the opening through the window.

"There's a way out through the bathroom window."

I stepped on the edge of the bathtub and carefully peeked my head through the window. I needed something to break out the rest of the glass so I ripped a hand towel from the broken rack hanging from the wall. I punched out the glass with my wrapped hand. I cleaned the shards of glass from the frame. As I peeked through the window, I tried to find the leverage to lift myself fully.

"I think it's clear," I looked back at Nicole. The car alarm drowned out the chaos. Outside the faint screams continued off in the distance.

I coaxed Nicole as I stretched out my hand, "Come on sweetheart. We have to go out the window." I reached for her hand as she slowly reached for mine. God she shook so badly!

I grabbed her hand, "Come on, you can do this! That's it sweetheart." Nicole looked out of the window at the desolate picture. She looked back at me, "Dad you should go first".

Nicole stepped back and I lifted myself through the window. Out where in my driveway nothing but fire was left. Burning chaos seemed to swallow the neighborhood. A police car screeched through the street, but the melted pavement popped its tires. The police car completely lost control and the rims created an indent into the neighbor's lawn. The front of the car popped up as it crashed into the neighbor's house. Flames consumed the police car. Sirens screamed around the neighborhood. What used to be a peaceful place was a burning chaotic war zone. Nicole and I paused in disbelief as we watched everything unravel right in front of us. I noticed my neighbor, Henry Chan, standing in front of his house. I waved my hand out the window to get his attention and prayed he could help us, but we were invisible. He just stood there taking in all the chaos, looking at it in complete shock. Streaks of fire lead up his lawn. The fire was so strong; a crackling blaze. His front lawn was torched and incinerated. With a blank, pale, empty look on his face, Henry Chan stood there trying to process all the chaos, unable to understand what was going on. Was it World War III? Was it the end of the world? The end of all life? A state of shock had Henry Chan frozen in time. I waved my hand back and forth through the window again. I hoped to get his attention.

"Henry! Help!" Nothing. We were still invisible; my voice was but a whisper amid the destruction and chaos. I wished I knew what was going on. As I caught Henry's attention, this look of emptiness shadowed over his face. Henry and I stared at each other as I continued to wave my arm for him to help us. He looked, but he just wouldn't move. He stood there, just staring at me as I waved him over from the small opening in the window. I paused in confusion as Henry slowly walked across his lawn. Streaks of fire smoldered through his lawn as he shuffled his feet. His focus on us was deep, but he walked through the flames like it was nothing; not an expression on his face. He continued over to the crumbled sidewalk and just as he was going to step out, a car zoomed past him, almost hitting him. Henry fell on his back as the car drove over his lawn, spitting dirt and fire into the air; ripping up the lawn that Henry had been so proud of. Everything was destroyed. We had to go. The stabbing pain in my side prevented me from having enough strength to move all the way and I fell back into the tub.

I looked up at Nicole, "I can't do it. You're gonna have to lift me Nicole. I need your help. Grab my foot."

Nicole grabbed my foot and assisted me out of the window. I slid my gut across the heated metal window frame. My body was like a dead fish flopping to the ground. Nicole quickly climbed out of the window behind me and tried to encourage me to move.

"Get up dad!"

My side had reopened; the blood juiced out of my side crippling me.

"DAD! GET UP! COME ON, WE HAVE TO GO!" Nicole said in a shaky, but urgent voice. Fuck, she was strong. I felt a twinge of pride as she pulled me up by the collar to help me to my feet. My arm wrapped around her shoulder; a crutch. I limped pathetically as she walked me to the middle of the street. The asphalt was melted to mush; heated to the point that we could walk no further. I turned, every direction, in disbelief. There were no words to describe the horror scene. We were in Hell. A Boeing 757 jet airliner crushed three houses, including mine. Fire and ash blew in the wind. The tail of the jet overtook what used to be my living room and garage. People were still alive; stuck in their seats, screaming for help, but burning alive. The smell of burning flesh filled the chaos. Nothing could be done. All we could do was watch. Fire from the jet fuel consumed the entire right side of the block. The jet fuel fed the flames as one man came bursting from the middle of the crash, burning alive with a tortured scream. The horror of it was shattering! The man screamed at the top of his lungs, begging for help, but I couldn't even make out what he was saying. The anguish was beyond enduring. The man ran around in circles. I continued to watch him, in horror, as he fell to his knees. The vivid image of it chilled my blood. We listened to this man burn alive, slowly, and finally fall to his face as his skin popped and crackled. He laid there, twitching and took his last breath.

My daughter and I stood there in pure and utter shock. The pit of my stomach sank. Off in the distance, fighter jets flew over the neighborhood streaking a concussion of sound piercing through the air; and a shock wave of vibration down to the ground. One right after the other they headed towards the city. To my left, I saw Jim, from down the street, covered in blood. His eyes were blood infused and he squeezed his fist, breathing through his teeth staring me down, hissing blood as saliva shot out of his mouth. He noticed Henry Chan standing there in fear with nowhere to go and nowhere to run. Jim sprinted as fast as he could, with no awareness that his left foot was on fire. He seemed completely incoherent to any pain as he sprinted at Henry; grabbing him with so much anger and violently throwing him to the ground. Jim punched and clawed at Henry's head. He smashed his head repeatedly into the ground. Henry's head bounced off the ground. Jim bit Henry's face. Blood painted the ground. Henry screamed and screamed for help. Jim finally took both thumbs and shoved them into Henry's eye sockets, popping his eyes. Henry's scream turned from a chilling, blood curdling scream to a whimpering moan as he squeezed Jim's arms blindly and took his last breath. Jim continued to beat and tear open Henry's lifeless body with a grueling anger. The sound of screams around the neighborhood cut through the sound of tires burning the pavement, police sirens wailed in unison with ambulances. The sounds of explosions fired off; gunshots echoed in surround sound.

8

The ash of the wreckage blew thickly in the wind. The fiery crash finished consuming my house. With the exception of Nicole, my whole world was gone. Jim stood to his feet and looked at Nicole and me. Blood dripped on his toes, his pajamas were soaked with Henry's blood. Jim's eyes pierced into mine. It was as though I could feel the hatred piercing my soul as he glared at me. He was like a lion when it needed to eat and hadn't for weeks. Through his teeth he let out a blood spattering hiss. With only seconds to react, Nicole and I sprinted as fast as we could, trying to get away. My wound forced me to lose my breath; I couldn't breathe. My sprint quickly turned into a slow jog from being unable to catch my breath. I could feel myself losing blood as my heart raced faster and faster; I was bleeding out. I could feel myself getting weaker and weaker. My attention landed on my neighbor, Alex's, cherry red 66" Chevy 4 door Impala sitting in his driveway.

"Nicole, we need to get to that car!" Jim instinctively sprinted at us. I'd never seen a 250 pound man run so fast. Nicole and I both leapt toward the car in a panic, bumping into each other, clumsily tripping over one another. Alex had left the window down, with the keys in the ignition. I opened the door and shoved Nicole into the passenger seat, but just as I was about to slide in, Jim viciously put a death grip on my wrist. He clawed and dragged me away from the car as I fought desperately to pull myself into the car. His hands slipped from the blood that coated them. He leapt on top of me which shoved me into the front seat. Jim did everything he could to inflict pain. He screamed and scratched at me, sneaking a couple punches; his blows hit me so hard I was seeing stars. I knew I didn't have the energy to fight him off. I knew I was at his mercy. I tried to kick him off. I didn't realize that I was so focused that my teeth were piercing my lip. We crushed against Nicole in the passenger seat as she shrieked, "Dad! GOOOOO!" I noticed the metal ice scraper on the floor, plunged my hand into Jim's throat and managed to gain enough leverage to reach the ice scraper. I squeezed the ice scraper tightly and plunged it into Jim's throat, popping the jugular. Blood squirted everywhere. It poured like a fire hydrant on my face and sprayed all over Nicole. It didn't even phase him. He persistently continued to claw at me and tried to bite the arm that kept the scraper lodged into his throat. The more he pushed at me the more it lodged deeper to the back of his throat. My thumb slipped into his jugular, restricting him from biting. His jaw chomped at me and he spat and hissed. I forced it into his eye over and over until his eye popped from the eye socket. I pulled the scraper out and with every ounce of strength I had left I stabbed over and over until he finally became lifeless. His heavy ass 250 pound body plopped on top of me. Nicole and I lifted him from my chest as blood still gushed from his neck. His limp, lifeless body crumpled onto the driveway. As I looked at him, a rage came over me and I jumped on top of him; raising the scraper I plunged into him repeatedly until all that was left of his head was a pile bloody, slushy mush. All this emotion and anger came over me. Anger consumed me. I screamed at the top of my lungs. I was pushed to my limits. I lost it. I was overwhelmed in my anger. I was exhausted and couldn't raise my arm when I came to my senses. I set my back against the car and sobbed. I broke down. My daughter looked at me like I was a monster; like she didn't know who anyone was anymore. She'd never even really heard me raise my voice. Terrified, her eyes welled. I used my sleeve to wipe the blood off my face; choking in disgust from the blood on my lips. I hoped that hadn't ingested any. as I worked to calm my heavy breathing. What I had just done was inhuman, but I suppose all my morals had gone out the window. I quietly and shamefully climbed into the driver seat. I gripped the steering wheel, trying to find any sort of reason for all of this chaos. I paused for a second to take a deep breath, reached out and twisted the key in the ignition. Alex sprinted suddenly out of his front door, following the sound of the engine. Alex stared us down with the same look as my wife and Jim. He furiously came our way, punching Nicole's window, his fist shattered the window. I didn't give anymore time to fight. I slammed the car into drive and sped out of Alex's driveway. He flung himself in through the back window, but the speed of the car ejected him when I turned. He refused to let go and I drug him alongside the car. I swerved the car left, then right, slamming my foot on the peddle, trying to shake Alex loose and avoid all of the vehicles that had stopped right in the middle of the road. Another car missed us by a hair as we crossed the first intersection. The engine roared, but Alex clung tightly; relentlessly. Alex tried to fight his way into the vehicle like a wild animal. His foot got caught under the tire and jerked him under the tire, crushing his foot up to his knee. Alex quickly grabbed onto the back bumper and dragged his body across the pavement, leaving a trail of blood and flesh painting the pavement. The car sped up faster and faster until Alex finally lost his grip; his body rolled away behind us. He got right back up and came after us, but the Impala had picked up enough speed to leave him behind. In the rear view mirror Alex slowly faded off in the distance. The car's back end fishtailed as I took a hard turn and drifted the back end into a light pole. Another crazed person jumped at the car and his body rolled over the back end of the car. The propulsion body slammed him across the pavement; his limp body rolled into the rear right end of another car and snapped his spine in half. He folded in half with the weight of the car and his heels kicked him in the back of the head. The car came to a complete stop as we collided into the pole, killing the engine. The impact threw Nicole into my right side, causing me searing pain as my wound reopened. Nicole scooted back across the seat to see Alex running from around the corner, bull rushing the backend of the car while the other crazed man slid his limp body towards the door; his bones twisted and crackled. Nicole noticed more and more of the crazed infected running at the vehicle from around the corner. More and more of them flooded around the corner. Nicole gasped as a flood of crazed people swarmed toward the car. I flicked the key back and forth, and the engine clicked, but nothing happened. We were stuck. We had no chance to run; sitting ducks with no way out. Nicole sat there looking back.

"They're coming!" she screamed in fear. "GO, DAD, GO!" In a panic I flicked the key back and forth again. Nothing. I realized it wasn't in park, threw it into 'p' and it finally turned over. The engine revved as I threw it into drive. I slammed my foot on the peddle, squealing the tires and disconnecting from the conjoined light pole. The Impala peeled out as twenty, or so, crazed infected men and women (even children) crowded the car. They crawled all over the car, like insects. On top of the vehicle they punched at the windows; doing anything and everything they could to get into the car and attack me and my daughter. One man smashed his fist into the back window, not caring that his hands were getting mangled. He pulled at the glass with his bare hands, ripping it apart as it crumbled like a cracker. Another worked to smash his face through the back window. He chomped his teeth, slammed his head into the window, mangling his face and successfully shoving it inside. Another burst through the windshield practically into Nicole's lap, where it was already weakened from other blows. He cut his chest and stomach on the broken glass; hissed and growled. He reached for Nicole's hair, grabbing a hand full, snapping her head forward. Nicole screamed for help! The swarm jumped and hurdled themselves like a net around the car. The car couldn't peel out because of the amount of bodies huddled on, and around, the car. More and more piled on top of us, crushing the car. The weight prevented the car from moving. More and more of them came. They ambushed the car. The engine revved as I slammed my foot into the pedal, overworking the engine. The harder I planted my foot on the pedal, the more the car would lower to the ground. The tire smoked up the car and the air around. I popped it from first gear to second to speed the car up. What was twenty infected quickly turned to fifty. Nicole screamed as the infected man pulled her hair. She struggled to fight him off. The car darkened from all the bodies climbing over the car. I punched the infected man as hard as I could. I grabbed his hand, trying to release it from Nicole's hair. I punched him and pushed until his hand tore away from Nicole's hair, taking a chunk of it with him. I pulled Nicole away from the window and pushed her down to the floor. I ducked my head and threw my body over Nicole as I slammed my foot on the peddle. I kept one hand on the steering wheel, hoping to somehow break away from the ambush of bodies that leapt onto the car. As it sped up, some of them fell off. I ran some of them over. The car picked up speed as the infected dropped off one by one. Nicole popped up from the floor to fight the one still hanging in the window. The car was catching speed quickly. Nicole jumped to the back seat so that she could kick the infected man. Her kicks worked and he slid back until he hung out the window by his fingertips. Nicole stomped the back of her heel, breaking each finger. Nicole's blows finally caused the man to tumble away. His limp body slammed into the pavement like a folding lawn chair, crushing his neck and skidding down the road. One hid on the top of the car and shoved his face inches from mine in the driver window. I tried to throw him off quickly by slamming my foot on the breaks. The front end of the car dipped and the tires shrieked.

"Hold on, Nicole!" I shouted as I stomped both feet on the brake pedal. The tires skidded down the road and in that split second on the right side of the car, a big red semi truck came blazing across the intersection. The grill of it plowed against the side, completely crushing the 66 Impala. The body of the lifeless infected man shot thirty feet into the air. His limbs split apart and rolled in separate directions. The road ripped his skin off. In that second, as the semi mutilated the front of the car, my wife's beautiful face suddenly flashed in my mind. I didn't know if it was from my head hitting the left side of the crushed window and door, or because I knew it was the end. The impact also threw Nicole's entire body into the left side of the back door, breaking her neck. The car flipped over and over; our bodies hurdled around in the car. It tossed me from the roof, back down to the seat; broken glass flew around the car. It felt like I was in a blender filled with razor blades being spun around in circles. Nicole and I were being thrown around like rag dolls. The car finally came to a dead stop from smashing into the liquor store on the corner of the street. Nicole and I both flew into the passenger side. The car was flipped on its top and for a split second, as I laid there, and still conscious, my entire body screamed in pain. I could feel the warmth of my blood dripping down my face. I'd felt weak. I'd lost too much blood. I called out to Nicole. I didn't get an answer. My eyes were getting heavy. I began to lose consciousness. My body weakened until I started to slowly fade away.

CHAPTER 2

Daylight's End

Startled, my eyes popped open in a panic. A loud gunshot rang. The world around us was still coming to an end. The chaos continued to unfold. My heart jumped in my chest the sound of the gunshot. It was so loud! My heart was beating frantically, my head pounded as I slowly came to, I could taste the blood pouring out of my mouth. The sharp pain in my side burned with furious pain. The wound had ripped wide open. My skin felt cold and clammy from the blood loss. I felt frozen; the warmth from my body gone. My muscles tightened. My head spun. I faded in and out of reality. My brain kept shutting down and rebooting. My eyes blurred, only to witness shadow movements around the car. The shadows passed through the light that peeked between the roof of the car and driver side door. Back and forth the shadows continued to move round the car, but my eyes wouldn't come back into focus. I couldn't tell what was going on. I saw a small light, so I blinked my eyes, hoping the more I did so, the quicker they would focus. I could hear tires shrieking as people passed by; gunshots popped off. When would it be over?I clutched at the wound on my side and struggled to remember why we were there in the first place.Finally, it dawned on me that the car had rolled multiple times. Images of the semi truck flashed in my head and I remembered Nicole was with me. It all rushed back to me. I needed to find Nicole. My eyes caught a small glimpse of her hair from behind the back seat. Light footsteps caught my attention. I laid there, silent, scared to shit. The shadow passed through the light between the roof and driver door. The footsteps crunched across the broken glass, dragging the glass underneath each foot step. I did everything I could to not make a sound. I tried my damndest to hold my breath, but I could feel the cough rolling up my throat. I was in too much pain. I closed my eyes and prayed that whatever it was would just go away. Then it crossed my mind that it could be someone to help someone who could rescue us. The shadow still paused next to the door. A shrieking sound came from behind the door followed by a hissing sound. I was in no shape or form to fight that thing off. I could make out the tip of a woman's high heel near the driver window. The hissing of the woman got louder and closer. The shadow between the roof got darker. The glass crunched louder and I noticed a knee crouching down. A bloody hand reached under, poking it's way through the small opening between the roof and driver door. I stopped breathing; the gangly, long fingernails wiggled around like they were trying to find something.

The hissing got louder while black blood droplets dripped onto the ground; the pavement and broken glass soaked it up. The long, gangly fingers wrapped around the top of the door. Manicured nails scratched at the leather interior. Dark brown hair lowered between the crack of the window. I couldn't handle another fight. Her teeth rattled, chomped her long fingers tugged at the door. Crusted blood encased her hands. She was right by my leg and she growled, deep and guttural. I could see her face. Suddenly, she stopped. She pulled her head up, her brown hair lifted from the ground; her fingertips took some of the leather from the door as she pulled away. Black ooze seeped into the car where she'd been. I pulled my leg away. I wasn't sure if that shit was contagious or not. The woman sprinted off; something else had caught her attention. A blood curdling scream roared off into the distance. I sighed in relief. I was light headed from trying to hold my breath. Her shrieking screams sounded distant. I couldn't move well, but I had to find Nicole.

My voice was hoarse. "Nicole...?" I coughed up blood and gulped air before calling out again. "Nicole?" "Sweetheart, where are you?"

I couldn't see. It was dark outside! How long had we been laying in the car? How long had I been passed out? The right side of my eye twitched as it gained focus; my left eye was swollen shut. I moved each muscle slowly, testing for strength and new pain. The windshield was shattered so badly it looked like a fog blanketed it. A brick wall had crushed in the passenger side like a soda can. I knew that I would have to go out the driver window and I was sick with terror. I had no idea if the infected woman, or any others were waiting in ambush. The coolness of the door panel actually felt good on my cheek as I slid out. Headlights beamed in my face from a car that had stopped right in the middle of the street. The driver side door was swinging back and forth. That meant more of those demons were still nearby. I tried to be silent as I slid through the sand box of broken glass. In a weakened tone, barely audible, I called for help. My voice was too soft and hoarse for anybody to hear, but I was afraid to get the wrong attention anyway. I scanned around, looking for human movement. The door of the car in the street slammed closed, scaring the shit out of me. As fast as I could I dragged my body back into the car.

I stared into the headlights and focused on a shadow passing over the headlights. A deep male voice spoke out, "Is someone there?" I tried to slide out to get his attention. I forgot all about the broken glass and blood. I realized that man was probably my only chance to save my daughter.

The voice called out again, "If you can hear me, I can help you."

"Yyyyesss! Wwwe are heeerree! Hhhellppp us. Pleeeasssse!" I tried to project my weak voice. I licked the dried blood off my lips. "Help!"

A dark shadow figure walked over to the car, kneeled down and peeked his head down into the window of the car.

"How many are in there?" His deep, raspy voice questioned from behind the door. "Have any of you been bitten?"

The question caught me off guard. Why would that matter? "Nnn...no. None of us were bitten, but I was stabbed and I've lost lots of blood." His huge black hand wrapped underneath the door.

"I'm gonna get you guys out. Hang tight!" Both of his hands gripped the door, tugging forcefully. "It's stuck. I need you to kick it from the other side as I pull." His dark voice felt reassuring.

I stuttered weakly stuttering, "I'm....ttt...tttooo...www...wweak. I'm sorry. I've lost a lot of blood."

"Hang on. I'll grab something to wedge the door open." A clunking crunching metal sound came from behind the door as the stranger tugged back and forth. The metal door squeaked, popped open and fell off its hinges. A tall, bulky black man with grey peppered hair stood at the door. The headlights shone around him like he was some kind of fucking superhero.

I sounded so small and petty when I tried to talk. "Dddamn! I'm glad ttt...ttt...to see you." Just before I reached my hand out, the woman who was at the door before came out of nowhere, lunging at our superhero, tackling him to the ground. Her shrieks and screams were a beacon to a crowd of the infected. From on top of him, the woman went straight for his jugular. He had no chance. She bit into his throat, pulling the meat and part of his esophagus out; blood spraying her in the face.

More and more of the infected jumped on top of him; one reached his hand in the top of his mouth, pulled his head back and savagely bit his face over and over. The hero screamed in sheer pain and agony. I laid inside the car in shock, watching them tear him apart. Blood curdling sounds came from his mouth.It was indescribable. Nothing could be done, but I felt like a coward as I pulled myself slowly back into the car and hid from them. More and more ran past the door like a herd of beasts, piling onto the man that was supposed to be our savior. All of them inflicted any type of pain possible. They slammed his head into the pavement over and over, cracking his skull into the pavement. And then, his screams were no more. The infected pulled him apart like it was a game. They obliterated him and scattered to prey on the next victim. I felt bad for the guy, but honestly, I was glad it wasn't me. I was hanging on to life as it was. A sense of shame and cowardice pumped through me. I tried to reassure myself there was nothing that I could have done. The footsteps were heavy and quick running around, screaming savagely. My thoughts were a jumbled mess of the images from throughout the day.

I silently twisted, scanning the dark vehicle for Nicole, hoping she would finally wake up and respond.

"Nicole...wake up I need to get you hh..help," I stuttered softly. "Wake up!" I saw her laying in a heap. "Sweetheart, we have to get out of here. I need you to wake up." I thought maybe we could sneak past the group of infected through the back or front windshield. "Nicole, get up babe. I think we can squeeze through the windshield." The possibility of her being dead began to grow heavy in my heart. "Nicole, sweetheart, wake up!" My eyes flooded with tears. No matter how I felt physically, it couldn't trump how I felt when the reality of losing my entire family hit me. I refused to believe it. My daughter had to be okay. My chin quivered, "Get up!" I laid in the car, silently sobbing my heart out. What had happened pierced back into my mind like a movie: the semi truck rolling through the intersection and t-boning us, the car bashing into the wall of the liquor store. It had all happened so fast. I just sobbed. I was defeated; ready to throw in the towel. The infected were welcome to come get me.

I slowly moved over, rolling over the glass as I slid my body across the glass on the roof of the car, using one arm after the other to get to Nicole. Crippling pain shot down my spine. "Nicole, wake up!" I slowly reached towards Nicole, my hand quivered and shook, cut up from the little shards of glass sticking out of it like a porcupine. Again, I spoke, "Nicole, wake up sweetheart. Come on, let's go..." I shuddered uncontrollably, my sobs heavy. I shook her, desperate for a response. "Dammit, Nicole, wake up....please, please...please...wake up!" Her lifeless body was still. I pulled her shirt, sliding us together. My heart began to sink down into my stomach. My daughter was dead...she was dead. I just stared at her as she laid there, her skin cold as ice. She'd probably been dead for hours. Blame set in. I blamed myself for every little thing. I could have saved her, but I was careless. It was my fault that the semi hit us. If only I would have just paid attention. I could have saved us both. Her long brown hair covered her face and a breath escaped her lungs. I was hallucinating. I had to be losing my damn mind. "Nicole?" She didn't move. I couldn't tell if she was alive. I leaned my back on the passenger door as more tears came, flooding my eyes. The biggest pain grew in my chest, or maybe it was a glimpse of hope. Whatever it was, it hurt worse than anything I had ever known. "Nicole, come on sweetheart, get up!" I grabbed her head and slapped her cheek. I had to wake her up. I shook her gently. "Nicole, God dammit! Wake up, please fucking wake up," I wailed.

I shook her again, "Nicole! Please, you have to wake up! I'm so sorry!" I begged God to let me take her place. I brushed her hair from her face. She had no expression in her eyes. Her bright green eyes looked dull; the sparkle she'd once had was long gone. Every father's worst nightmare was my reality. I'd lost my entire family in one day. I held my baby girl tightly in my arms, rocking back and forth. Nicole was cold. Her hands were ice. I think we sat there for what seemed to be hours, but was probably only seconds. I was completely detached from the chaos that unfolded outside of the car. Time meant nothing. There was nowhere to go. I just wanted to sit there and hold my child while I sang her favorite song, the one I used to sing to her when she was a kid.

"Please don't go away, but if you do, I'll go with you forever; loving you forever, holding you. I never want to let you go. Hold my hand and take me along with you and I'll never lie. I'll be true to you, promise my heart won't go blue." We rocked and I sang; my tears fell on Nicole's face. I stroked her hair. Suddenly, I felt her arm twitch. I froze. I didn't know what to feel. She was too cold and stiff to be alive. How could she have been alive after all that time with no sign of breath? I moved her cautiously and gently; her neck made a small twitch, the bones in her neck cracked and twitched. Her jaw popped open, letting out the most chilling moan. Her teeth chattered. The air trapped in her lungs blew out. I felt the cool air brush my face.

Her middle finger slowly moved and she squeezed her hand into a fist, making a popping sound with her knuckles. Her fist began to rattle violently. The more she moved, the louder the crunching and crackling of her bones got. It was like her muscles forced her broken bones to move. The left side of her body moved slowly. Her arms curled inward, gaining momentum, shaking violently. Her teeth chattered like they were going to break. I pushed back from me gently.

I spoke softly, "Nicole?"

She let out another chilling, gurgling moan that sent chills down my spine. Her once bright green eyes were infused with blood. Her arm violently flew up and with intense precision she grabbed a big chunk of my hair and growled in my face. She pulled me down towards her with ease. With ferocious hisses she tried to get my neck into her mouth. I resisted, but I was too weak. Her body stiffened just before she bit into me. She was having a seizure, puking; blood mixed with black stomach bio projected violently. My heart sank as I realized that I was going to have to fight someone else that I loved. I grabbed her hand and forced her to rip a chunk of hair out of my head. She still didn't fully release me. I aggressively pushed and kicked her off of me, but fell backwards, hitting my head on the top of the passenger seat. We wrestled in the tight space the car provided. The shadows outside of the car came to a complete stop. I crawled my way back under the passenger seat from the back of the car to the front. A crowd of infected turned their focus onto the commotion in the car. From my angle our gazes all met. Nicole clawed and scratched her way from behind the bench seat. She catapulted her entire body at me, clenching her jaw shut, scratching at my legs. Her shoulder got stuck between the roof of the car and the bench seat. I knew it wouldn't hold her for long. The group of infected rushed to get in the car. A three hundred pound man, like a rhino, led the pack and threw himself into the car door. Hands clawed their way around him, sticking their dozen, or so, flailing arms around his fat body. Nicole's shoulder popped loose from the seat. Her arms shot at me. Without hesitation, stopping her dead in her tracks, I did what anyone would have done in that situation and brutally stomped my foot into her forehead; her already broken neck popped and cracked with every stomp. With everyone stomp, Nicole writhed and twisted, goo dripping profusely from her ferocious mouth. While I fought Nicole off, I happened to notice the small opening between the shattered windshield and the roof of the car. It took a couple of pushes as I jabbed my elbow to widen the opening. The fat reached for me, but his stubby ass arms were too short. He was stuck. It was Nicole that I had to worry about. Nothing phased her enough to stop her relentless attack. Her teeth caught the bottom of my pants, almost taking a chunk out of my leg. Nicole's neck was twisted and broken, preventing her head from being stable enough to get a bite out of me. Her head bounced around only being held by the skin of her neck. Her neck was broken, but her grip was tight. The more I struggled to get away from her, the more aggressive and powerful she became. Her nails dug deep into my skin and peeled it down to my ankles. With one final blow, I kicked her in the head. It twisted in a complete 180, snapping back, breaking what was left in her neck, her head pushing the spine through the back of her neck . She dragged her body around the roof of the car by her arms. I was free to get through the windshield, but I could hear Nicole still scratching at the top of the roof, ripping the liner. My heart pounded, tears streamed down my face. I couldn't breathe. I couldn't explain the amount of physical and emotional pain I was in. I gave one last glance back at Nicole as she chattered her teeth at me. I slouched down against the brick wall and hid from all the infected on the other side of the car. The frog lingered in my throat. I pulled the big chunks of broken glass out of my chest and legs. I thought I was going to black out from the pain. The battle was over. I was defeated. Broken. Beaten to a pulp, sobbing like a little bitch. I thought adrenaline was supposed to mask the pain but I felt every second of it. A strong roll of thunder crashed above, rain droplets began sprinkling. Fuck, that day just got better and better. Rain poured harder and harder by the second, quickly turning into a monsoon. The ground flooded vastly. It hadn't rained that hard in months. Why then? Lightning illuminated the faces of the infected who suddenly looked lost and confused. I figured it was all God's way of sending "a fuck you" message to the world, complete with a P.S. "Go fuck yourself". Rightfully so considering that the world and all morals had gone to utter shit. The rain washed my blood soaked face and body. I felt amused for a moment. I leaned against the brick both defeated and relieved. I closed my eyes and the coolness of the rain calmed me. Nicole's hand grabbed at my leg. When I looked down at her, I was almost at peace for a moment. Her hand pulled at me, but not in a violent way that time, more like she was in need. My heart shattered. It was almost like she was pulling at me like she needed her dad, but I knew that wasn't reality. It wasn't my Nicole that reached for me; that wasn't my little girl. I released her hand and she moved through the flood water, looking lost just like the others. I found the strength to climb to my feet. The infected wandered around, unaware of me being there. It was like the rain had them distracted. The wound in my side shot down through my hip, dropping me to my knees. I was crippled by it and it prevented me from going anywhere. My stomach felt twisted, my ribs began convulsing. I threw up blood. My stomach squeezed, pushing everything out until I could only dry heave; my stomach wanted to push its way through my mouth. My throat closed like it was getting rung out like a towel. Then suddenly I stopped choking on my own blood and coughing, so I rolled over onto the pavement to let the rain beat my face. Death knocked at my door. I had no idea how I'd survived so long.

When my eyes opened, hundreds of the infected stood around me in the parking lot. The sound of the rain hit the ground so violently, muffling the sound of my movement. They were completely unaware of my existence. I kept my head on a swivel as I stood in the middle of the battle ground. Heads of the infected twisted and snapped back, one right after another. A small, gangly, homeless man caught my attention. He looked off, different from the rest; like he had been beaten to shit for a hundred years. His clothes hung, ripped and torn off his body. My eyes scanned him up and down. Something about him scared the shit out of me. The meat of half of his face was missing, hanging off the bone. His hand reached up to separate the chunk of flesh hanging off his face; tossing it to the ground like a child would with food it didn't want. The eye on his left side pulled from the socket leaving a gaping hole in his dismembered face. That small homeless man snarled at me, showing his teeth, his neck twisting back almost in a 180 degree motion. All of the infected hissed and came to a charging stance, coordinating their attack on me. 'Fuck', I thought to myself. They surrounded me. The homeless man screamed and lunged at me. Scared, I dropped to my knees, causing the homeless man to over shoot me. He splattered across the ground.I couldn't get traction and I stumbled as I tried to get back up. One of my feet finally got a grip, but it was too late. Another of the infected bull rushed me with his shoulder, planting it into my left side.

    My entire body flew into the wall of the liquor store. The infected man charged head first into the wall, a cracking sound came from his head and it bounced off the wall. Another infected stared me down, never losing eye contact. It was the fat fuck from the car. I left our stare down to sprint away from his big ass bear claw of a hand, but it wrapped around the back of my neck squeezing tightly, lifting me from behind and slammed me into the brick wall. I twisted my neck to look at the fat fuck. He grinned at me like he knew I was going to be his little bitch. His stomach protruded like it couldn't even contain his fat. Then, finally, it tore, and his guts unfolded. From his fat fucking body his stomach and intestines poured and tumbled. His intestines dragged in the mud, but he was unphased. The rest of the infected looked to be on standby, like he was the leader of the pack. They were waiting for him to make his kill. It was almost like all of them were in sync, standing by, waiting to charge at me. The fat man's feet stomped on his intestines as they unraveled out of his stomach, tripping him. Next in line. Another infected man swung his tongue back and forth and quickly charged at me. I stepped back slowly, frozen in fear, nursing my side. The wall was the only thing holding me up. The infected continued to charge at me. I tried to move, but I needed the wall and I slipped in the mud. One of them lunged at me, her heels sinking into the mud at the same time that I lost my footing. Some of them jumped into the wall, some jumped into each other like savages, one jumped over me missing me by a hair. My feet were unable to gain grip in the muddy water. Another one grabbed a hold of my shirt pulling the tail. He quickly lost his grip; everything was too wet and muddy. I was on my back, I couldn't get up and the mud penetrated my wounds. I resorted to slithering across the mud. Another one of the infected jumped on top of me, struggling to get a grip on me. He held my face in the mud water. Every time I tried to breathe, I sucked up muddy water. My face pressed into the muddy water. I added drowning to the list of ways that I was going to be taken out. Thank God for the mud, though, because the man slipped off of me and I was able to lift myself up from the ground. I slipped and slid all over running towards the flipped 66 Impala. That damn car was my only protection, but it was too late. They all knew I was there. They all knew I had nowhere to go.

All of them chased after me with one goal: kill Randy Stollstheimer. The only thing between them and me was the Impala. There was just enough space for me to squeeze through to hide. I threw myself behind the car as one of them leaped after me; his shoulders too wide to fit between the space of the car and the wall. His hand reached the tip of my toes. I felt another of them grabbing at my feet and legs. I looked down, remembering that Nicole was still trapped in the car. Her body hung halfway out of the car, her hair still caught in the windshield rendering her unable to bite me. The crowd fought and struggled with each other to get to me. They came at me from every direction, but I was tucked away just enough. Then, BOOM: a gunshot rang out, echoing throughout the small space. The sound bounced off the wall, piercing my ear drums, both of my hands immediately shot up to cover my ears. My ears rang; I couldn't hear at all. My head began spinning making, me somewhat incoherent. I immediately felt like slow motion was in effect. White flashes appeared behind the infected. One right after the other dropped. I looked to my right, the infected men and women swung their arms at me fiercely, another man's head exploded, his limp body falling to the ground, clogging the hole one right after the other. I curled into the fetal position between the car and the wall, just waiting for it to be over. I think I was screaming at the top of my lungs. My head spun. I felt a hand grab my shirt and pull me into the opening between the store and car that was crushed from the crash. I hadn't seen it before. The hand pulled me through the store wall tossing me into the store. I fell to my knees on the wet, slippery tile floor. The store was pitch black. I was unable to see who was doing the shooting. BOOM: flashes lit up the store. Each bang brought the infected down into a pile of death. Gunshots echoed throughout the store. I had no idea what was going on. More and more: BOOM, BOOM, BOOM. My head rang from each blast. It was too dark in the store to even see what was going on. Two dark shadows emerged from the darkness. Their voices in sync. It was still hard for me to make out what they were saying; their voices were muffled. I faintly heard the locks on the door snap. I squinted to focus on the door. The store blacked out the shadows of the infected, but I heard them pounding on the windows. The liquor store had barred windows which prevented anyone from bursting through the glass. Though, some of them hung on the bars like wild monkeys. One right after the other they charged at the welded bars on the doors and windows. Some belligerently slammed their faces into the bars and then dropped. Dead bodies piled so high next to the car that they plugged the hole in the wall. The majority of the infected pounded against the door in front of the store. The hinges on the door bent and moaned as the door frame started to give way. Everything happened so fast! The door shook ferociously. They wanted to get in and they were going to get in. The door fame splintered apart as the door slammed to the ground. A flood of infected forced their way in all at once, getting clogged up in the small opening. Shots continued popping off. A hand grabbed me on the back of my collar, pulling me across the muddy, wet tile. The gun was inches from my head as each gunshot went off. Whoever it was dragged me through the aisle of the liquor store. I couldn't hear. I made out a faint voice yelling at me to get the fuck up. I was too wet and slippery; unable to my feet.

A man's deep voice hollered next to my ear, "Get the fuck up, dumbass!"

The hand on the back of my collar yanked me up forcefully. I grabbed the shelf next to me to steady myself. Flashes and glimpses of the ravenous faces got closer. A crippled, mangled hand reached for me, almost touching my face. Both of my hands white knuckled the shelf. Whoever was helping me was strong as fuck because he had a death grip on me and I felt like I was being dragged like a little girl. My hands were easily ripped away from the shelf. Mr.Ninja Death Grip squeezed his fingertips into my shoulder. I could feel his fucking fingernails piercing the skin. The flood of the infected bulldozed their way through the liquor store, sounding like an angry mob. Dozens of them screamed at the top of their lungs. They pounded through the store, knocking over bottles. My heart raced. It sounded like they were right behind us. Chills shot down my spine like a knife stabbing my back. I stumbled to keep up with Mr. Ninja Death Grip. The infected crushed each other as they rushed down the aisles. One of the infected narrowly missed the left side of my face. The outline of Mr. Ninja Death Grip appeared in the shadows next to me as he yanked me out of the way. The infected man missed me by a hair and fell into the boxes of liquor bottles that filled the storage room. The exit door in the back of the liquor store burst wide open. Two big hands tossed me out through the back door into the alley.

With a tremendous amount of force, I landed on my back in the alleyway, cracking my forehead on a dumpster. The heavy rain continued to pour; lightning and thunder took over the sky. I bit my tongue and rolled over the soggy bags of trash near the dumpster. Mr.Ninja Death Grip fought off the infected inside of the liquor store. It was my chance to run. I tried to roll my ass out of the pile of trash bags. This was my chance to run, but my conscience got the better of me, urging me to help him. I stared at the black hole in the middle of the door. It fell silent and then the back door opened with a clanging BOOM! A gunshot lit up the back room. I had no idea where the other man had gone. He must've gotten taken by the infected. Mr. Ninja Death Grip could handle it. I was barely living. There was no way I could help him. A brutal scream roared out from the darkness. A gigantic man jumped out of the darkness, through the rain, in a police uniform, slamming into the front of the dumpster and then into the planks of the wooden fence next to it. The police officer bounced off the dumpster into a shooting stance and shot into the darkness, blasting anything that moved. Watching this guy move around was like something out of a Rambo movie. I didn't know what to do. It was all so quick.

Suddenly, his deep Stallone voice shouted, "Get the fuck up! What's the matter with you, asshole?" He grabbed my arm and pulled me to my feet, yet again, dragging me through the alley by my arm. The police officer sprinted down the alley, dragging me like an idiot behind him. Honestly, I was kind of pissed that I was being manhandled by this cop.

We ran to the end of the alley toward his police car. He popped the clip from his 9mm and loaded a new one. His head didn't even turn back to the infected that poured out of the back door of the liquor store. He aimed and shot backwards. I glanced back, watching the infected drop like flies. Fuck, this guy didn't even looked back and he was still accurate. He popped his trunk and pulled out an AR-15. This guy was calm, like he knew what the fuck he was doing. He pulled a cigar from the breast pocket of his shirt. Infected rolled down the alley, getting closer and closer, sprinting towards the car. The officer calmly lit his cigar and aimed his AR-15. BOOM, BOOM,BOOM...Bullets sprayed through the alley, whistling through the air, heads exploded. The spray of bullets dropped the infected to the ground. The last shot that came out went through one head, right into another, stopping both of them. I thought to myself, 'This guy is good. Who the fuck is this guy?'

Before I knew it, he had me by the arm again and shoved me into the back of his car. I flopped into the back seat while he slammed the door behind me. Who the hell did this guy think he was? The rain pounded, making visibility impossible. The rain flooded over the windows. I couldn't see what the hell was going on. It was quiet, not a sound coming from the outside of the car, then suddenly a shrieking scream echoed, followed by a loud blast. I tried to wipe the condensation to see what was happening. I reached through the darkness to open the door.

"Fuck it's locked," I snapped to myself. I was stuck. Silence filled the air before gunshots continued popping off, lighting up the back window. A shadow ran past the left side of the car. I was completely unable to see what was going on, but the door finally opened. The police officer tossed his AR into the passenger seat of the car and hopped in. Just when he was about to close the door, one of them leapt on top of him. He shoved his hand into the neck of the infected woman, giving her a swift head butt, cracking her forehead wipe open and slingshotting her head backwards. Without hesitation, he shoved his 9mm pistol into her jugular, popping a couple shots off. The bullets flew out of her neck. The pink mist of her blood painted his face and the inside of the car. The shots were not even coming close to phasing her. He shoved his forearm into her throat, pinning her head to the roof of the car, pressing the gun tightly to her forehead. The woman struggled and clawed at his arm, violently punching him in the face. He pinned her to the roof of the car with his forearm, slowly pulling the trigger like he got some joy out of it. The bullet blasted through her head, into the steel of the car. She went limp and Mr. Ninja Death Grip kicked her off. Another one leapt on him. They wrestled in the front seat. The officer shot the infected in the stomach and the bullets exited through his spine. I actually felt safe in the back of the cop car. Ninja Death Grip killed the infected like it was an everyday job for him.

It was impossible to even see this guy's face. Every time I got a chance, something would happen, or block his face. It was steamy and too dark for me to see much of anything. Every time he got rid of one crazy lunatic, more jumped in. Two or three jumped on the back of the car. One of them slammed his head into the back window repeatedly until the window splintered. The police officer started the car, continuing to get every shot off at each body jumping at him. He threw the car into drive, smashing his foot on the pedal. The engine of the car vibrated the entire car. The driver side door remained open as one of them clung to it. The car gained speed down the alleyway, scraping against the walls of the alley. The officer swiped the car back and forth against the walls to shake the infected from the car. More and more of the infected jumped on top of the car. Mr.Ninja Death Grip slammed the car into reverse. The bodies of the infected pounded against the back end of the car, almost sounding like the torrents of rain. Mr. Ninja Death Grip threw the car into drive again, smashing gears and hauling ass down the alley once again. The fuckers would just not let go.

The sound of the bones crunching, along with metal scraping, made my skin crawl. Blood from the grinding bodies joined the rain and washed over the car. Bodies were splitting in half as the car bashed them into the walls. I'm sure he couldn't see where he was going, either. The police officer stomped his foot on the gas. The car had gained momentum, sparks flew everywhere. I was terrified. I started to scream. The police officer told me to shut the fuck up or he couldn't concentrate. I couldn't help myself. I was broken. All the things I'd been through had built up and were pouring out of me in the form of screams. The police officer squeezed the steering wheel tightly, pulling it to the left and then to the right, trying to gain control of the car. The wiper blades slashed through the puddle of water and blood. It was impossible to see out. Just as the car emerged from the alley, ten or so of the infected came sprinting around the corner, taking on the cop car head on. Most ended up getting smashed under the tires, or sliding off, but one bashed his head right through the windshield. His body hanging halfway in the windshield, halfway out. I freaked out and screamed at the top of my lungs. More and more of them charged the car, using their bodies to smash into the metal. You could hear their skulls crunching against the car. The cop car blazed through the mob, the nose of the car bouncing up and down into the air. A flood of bodies rolling under the front of the car. The speed and momentum of the car rocketed the car into the air, slamming my entire body up into the roof of the car, then slamming me back down. The infected man hung out of the middle of the windshield and continued to attack the police officer. The car slammed into the rear end of a parked car. Mr. Ninja Death Grip punched the infected as he peeled the car away from the wreck. He went into reverse, then drove forward at top speed and hit the parked car again. I slammed into the window dividing the front from the back. The force of the accident tossed the infected into the rear end of the other car. The cop car came to a complete stop. The horn stuck blaring and attracting more of the infected. The rain constantly poured into the front of the car through the gaping hole in the windshield. The police officer tried to catch his breath after his chest had slammed into the steering wheel. The police officer attempted to start the car. The engine chugged to turn over, but the car stalled every time. Two of the infected jumped in the front window. The cop instinctually pulled his gun out, shooting one in the head and the other in the chest. the infected men fell backwards from the hood of the car. Shooting more infected and jamming the gas pedal down, Mr. Ninja Death Grip tried everything to get the car started. The car finally started, but there were so many infected clinging to it.

    The police officer fired gunshots into the roof of the car, not caring what he hit, before speeding off. He sped away with such haste that he kept crashing into parked cars on the side of the street. The flood of infected that attempted to get into the car were shot, the rest chased behind us. Smoke from the engine emerged and mixed with rain, blocking the sight of the cop. Smoke flooded the cab of the car and the officer attempted to clear the smoke and rain by waving his hand. As the smoke partially cleared, we both realized that the road was blocked off by an abandoned military blockade. As he attempted to bring the car to a halt, it hydroplaned and lost control. We crashed into a tank and completely totaled the front end of the car. The engine and transmission pushed its way into the cab of the car with the impact of the crash, slamming the cop into the steering wheel, knocking him unconscious and pinning him where he was. My entire body flew into the glass guard, knocking the wind out of me. I could feel all the bones in my body popping. I gasped for air, trying to get the attention of the cop, unaware of the hundreds of infected that flooded to the car, following the blaring horn beacon. I tried to scream at the officer and weakly slammed my fists against the glass guard.

I gasped, "Hey! Wake the fuck up!" I threw myself down on the seat, kicking the bullet proof guard window in between the seats as hard as I could to wake him up. "Get the fuck up!" Shadows of bodies got closer and closer, running, pounding their bodies on top of the car. The weight of them crushed the roof of the car; the back window popped.

I was trapped. There wasn't any way out of this. We were trapped and the car was surrounded. I was stuck in the back seat with nowhere to go. I had no choice but to continue kicking the glass shield as hands started to reach into the windows, scratching and clawing at me. I slid my way into the middle of the seat as I attempted to kick the window, screaming with the hope that this guy would wake up. The flood of infected climbed their way into the car. A group of infected reached in, pulling the unconscious body of the police officer out of the front windshield, brutally pulling him apart. They tore him into fleshy pieces in a matter of seconds. They ripped the skin on his face, digging bloody fingertips into his eyes, detaching them from the membranes of his head. Some of the infected noticed I was in the back seat of the car and jumped in the front seat. Unable to break the glass guard, they hissed and growled at me violently. I couldn't even see the officer any more. It looked the infected had consumed the entire police officer in the matter of seconds. My heart sank knowing this was probably the end. I didn't have any more chances or random saviors. The back window began cracking more and more, finally shattering. Water rushed in and I felt like I was drowning. The infected reached in through the back window. There was nowhere to go. With one last ditch effort, I threw myself on the floor, pushing any hands away from me, kicking anything that moved. One of the infected grabbed my arm and I felt its teeth sink in, biting a chunk of flesh from the side of my arm, pulling muscle tissue apart. One of the infected grabbed a hold of my left leg, the fingernails peeled my flesh back to the bone. It pulled and bit through my leg muscles; teeth clenched my toes as the bones in my feet disassembled. Teeth sunk into my entire body as they pulled me through the window. Teeth sunk into my neck. It was agony...I felt them as they dug through my stomach. A hurricane of fists continued to pound my face, my head violently bouncing off the back of the car. I felt my skull crack and crunch until I couldn't move anymore. I was paralyzed. My body wouldn't move, but I could feel every torturous second.

CHAPTER 3

Officer Tommy Maestas and Officer Erik McAllister

I thought coming out of the police academy I'd be the next big, badass fucking cop. The next John McClain or John Wick. At the academy I'd had the fastest running records and even had the best shooting record plaque on the wall of fame. Once I'd gotten assigned to the police station out in District 6, I was pretty confident that I'd have the golden fucking carpet laid out for me. Boy, was I in for a surprise as I strolled into the Chief's office the first time. He sat there quietly, with a toothpick in his mouth, chewing it back and forth, sucking back the spit on the edge of his mouth. The stench of coffee and cigar consumed the air as he clicked his pen over and over. His eyes bounced back and forth from me, to the file he had in his hand. I sat there quietly waiting for him to say something. To be honest, I was kind of nervous. Word around the Academy was that this guy was a hard ass and if you said the wrong thing, he flew off the handle. He'd assign his best officers to scrub the shitters without hesitation. He sat there, sucking on the toothpick in his mouth, not saying a damn word, just staring at me. Then he opened his mouth, sucking back the spit off the toothpick, and took a deep breath. Silence fell again. The sound of his desk clock ticking coupled with

CASTLE CAGE

the click of the pen. Nothing. He looked at me like he could see into my soul.

He finally cleared his throat to speak in a high pitched voice, "So... you think you're a hot shot cadet?"

"No sir," I replied in a modest tone. The truth was that I knew I was going to be the baddest mother fucker they had ever seen come out of the academy.

He spit the toothpick onto his desk, "Shut the fuck up! Did I fucking ask you to speak?"

I stared at him, confused. I wasn't sure if he was joking, or not, but he sat there, straight faced. The skin on his face hung like a bulldog and with a smug look on his face, he squinted his eyes at me. I stared back and twirled my thumbs.

"Well, no sir. I'm here to prove that I'm the best, sir!"

There was no expression on his face. The wrinkles on his face aged deeply into his skin. I don't think you could tell if this mother fucker was smiling or not. I thought to myself, 'Fuck this asshole. I will show him. He'll be sorry he ever doubted me.'

I see mother fuckers like you come out of the academy like hookers shooting babies out of their pussies."

Honestly, I giggled a little because he had full faith in what he was saying.

"Are you laughing at me, Dick Skin?" He slammed his fist on the desk, his face turning red, as he questioned me. He was fucking pissed at the world and I rolled in to take the dick sandwich the dude was ready to dish out.

I lifted my eyebrow, cocking my head back as I responded, "Well, sir, my report should show that I'm the best to come out of my class, sir!"

He snapped back at me, "I don't give a fuck if you're Shirley fucking Temple whistling somewhere over the rainbow out of your ass hole, Cock Face!"

The Chief had a colorful way of putting words together. It was just as good as the fucked up wardrobe he was wearing, with the tip of his shirt hanging out of his zipper. He stood up from his desk and walked around his office. It was hard not to look at it, but there it was.

"Sir you're...ummm.. zipp..."

Before I could finish the sentence he slammed both hands on his desk, staring me down.

"Did I ask you to talk, Fuck Nuts? You just don't comprehend, do you? You a little slow, boy?"

I was starting to get the routine. He was the hardass Chief, ready to squish anyone underneath him.

"Sir, your shirt is stuck in your zipper, sir!"

He looked down at his zipper, then back at me and his face turned deep red. He fumbled with his zipper, struggling to free the shirt from the zipper. As he freed his shirt, he took a deep breath, his face deep red with embarrassment.

With my folder in hand, he shouted, "Get the fuck out!" and then called out to one of the other officers, "Stone! Show Captain America to his desk." As we walked to my new desk, I noticed that a lot of the desks were empty.

2

It seemed unusual to see so many missing officers. I followed the police officer. He kept leading me down more and more stairs, farther and farther away from the prime desk locations, until we were in the actual basement. The fucking basement. That shit was barely lit. It looked a damn morgue.

Officer Stone walked down the hallway and chuckled, "Man, what did you do to piss the chief off?"

I looked back at Stone with a passive look on my face. I wanted to punch the asshole, but I held back, grinding my teeth.

Through clenched teeth, I responded, "Nothing!"

Stone smiled at me, "Fine. Sorry I asked. Here you go, Sunshine." I slammed my stack of folders on the small desk in the darkest corner behind the double black doors. The light above flickered. I swear you could smell the mold growing. I felt like I was just dropped a shit bomb of fucking humble pie. I was assigned to the smallest desk, in the smallest police station in Denver, Colorado. I took a deep, disappointing breath of moldy air. The desk shook and wobbled with the weight of my folders. It felt like if I ever tried to put a cup of coffee on that bitch it would fall to pieces. I'd never been so pissed in my life. My face felt bright red and my ears burned with fury.

I was supposed to be the cool kid, big man on campus. But, I wasn't at all. I was the schmuck in the basement, filing papers and logging evidence. As the days went by, the depression kicked in. I couldn't help but to think to myself how much I hated walking through the police station, like a fucking pathetic fool, while everyone watched me go to work in the dungeon. All the action was happening on the outside and I was stuck on the inside pencil pushing. Maybe I was being a whiny little bitch, but I was fucking bitter. On that particular day, though, everything was different. That day would change everything, forever. Just like every other day, I grabbed my stack of folders and pathetic excuse for a cup of coffee and made my way to my desk. When you first walked in, on the right side, the very first desk was smaller than mine. I thought mine was bad. It was only four feet wide and stood to the hip of the female officer standing behind it. Officer Ronda Lopez was a short Mexican chick, tiny as all hell. She would go out of her way just to say hi to me every morning. She wasn't too bad; she was actually very pretty, but I wasn't interested. Every morning she would ask me when we were going to grab a drink, or flirtily ask me where her donuts and coffee were. It didn't matter what time of day it was, she was always in the mood to flirt with me. I kind of got tired of hearing it, so every morning I woke up 30 minutes early just to make it to the donut shop down over on Hampden. Officer Lopez was picky; the only donut she would eat had to be the pink sprinkled kind. She said it always reminded her of her favorite TV show. I was never a fan of watching TV. I never had a clue what show she was talking about. She would quote lines from it to cheer me up. Every morning before my shift, I'd hit the gym to get the frustration of the dead end job off my shoulders. I never got to go out on calls, not even a ride along. My parents and family were proud of me that I chose to go to the academy to become a police officer; what a fucking letdown.

I didn't have the guts to tell my dad that my job title was: Basement Desk Bitch. My mom already told everyone back at home that I was the golden child. I just couldn't tell them that I was stuck in a dark basement, filing the papers like I was scum of the earth. Freaking John McClain stuck in the damn basement. No one ever even came down to see me. Lopez wouldn' t even go down there. She said it smelled like a wet dog's ass down there.

As I walked by, I overheard the Chief talking to Stone about Officer Maestas and how he was transferring from uptown to help with the shortage of cops. I overheard that Maestas was a real John McClain type and that we were lucky to have him on the force. It sounded like Officer Maestas was one badass mother fucker. God, I was bitter! If they needed help so bad, why the fuck was I stuck in the Goddamn basement? I peeked in through the cracked open door and heard the actual smug look on his face. Right away, I thought to myself, 'Fuck you, Chief'. A tap on my shoulder thumped hard enough to push me into the door head first, breaking up the conversation between Chief Morrison and Officer Stone.

"McAllister! What the hell are you doing? Don't you know how to fucking knock?" Both of them stared at me through the awkward silence.

Two heavy footsteps walked in shortly after me. Chief Morrison placed both hands on his hips "Ah! Officer Maestas! Come in! We were just talking about you." He smiled from ear to ear, reaching his hand out to greet the superhero. I turned my head slowly to see the ass hole standing behind me. His big bear claw sized hand reached out to meet Chief Morrison's.

"Damn I'm glad to see you, Maestas" the Chief squeaked in his high pitched voice. "Stone, show Officer Maestas to his desk." My head slowly turned back to look at Maestas. My eyes met the middle of his chest and had to roll up to get to his face. He was huge.

Chief Morrison squeaked again, "Come see me after you get settled in and we can catch up." I felt the intimidation roll in as our eyes met. Maestas turned around and walked away.

Chief Morrison glared at me. "McAllister. What the fuck are you still doing here?". He shook his head at me. "Get the fuck out and get to work, dumbass." Stone walked cautiously out after Officer Maestas. Chief Morrison yelled after me, "Shut the fucking door!"

I slammed the door behind me, the door knob punching me in the ass cheek shoving me forward. Officer Lopez walked up with a sexually aggressive look on her face, watching Maestas walk by.

"Who is that?" she asked, biting her lip as she undressed Officer Maestas with her eyes. I looked back at her, "What the Fuck?"

Lopez gave a snarky look, her eyebrow lifted, rolled her eyes and said, " I'm not yours, am I?" She walked away from me shaking her hips confidently. The officers sitting at their desks followed her with their eyes. Dicks. I marched down to the basement in frustration slamming the stack of folders on my desk.

As time passed everyone constantly congratulated Officer Maestas on his drug bust or high speed chase take down. Out of all the officers that would never come down, Officer Maestas would always come down and say hi. He always had a reason to be down there; dropping off evidence or making me file his reports. I hated his ass, but after a while he was the only one who would talk to me. All the others would spit in my coffee, or push my papers off the desk. We eventually kind of became friends. He was the best cop on the force, but somehow he was never too cool to talk to the quiet guy stuck down in the basement. Every day I would ask him, "When am I going to get to go out and see some action?"

His answer was always the same. "Really, Erik, you have a good job down here. You're the lucky one." He'd give me a smirk as he walked away. The days went more and more slowly. I'd catch myself staring at the clock, watching the second hand go around.

3

Officer Bill Tandy would come in to release me from my shift. He was an older guy. He was about to turn 67 and had a wife and all his kids moved on to college. He was a real quiet guy. He was also a face talker; always coming in to work with his breath smelling like sardine sandwiches. Everyday he ate the same lunch: sardines and coffee. He didn't give two shits that his breath smelled like sardines and coffee. I'd get stuck every day for about 30 to 40 minutes hearing how he'd met Elvis Presley, the king of rock and roll, and how they'd had coffee together all the time when they were both enlisted in the army. He would always say he and Elvis were the best of friends. When the clock hit between 7 and 8, I expected Bill to come in. He was a no show; not even a phone call. Nothing. Usually he was early. I always thought that if he could have, he would've lived here. Bill hated being home. Bill never missed a day of work.. It was his only way to get away from his wife . He would call his wife the beast . It was really unusual that he wasn't there, so I decided to call and check in. The phone just rang and rang. I couldn't get any answer. It went to voicemail after ringing. Officer Maestas walked past the black double doors, leaving from the middle of his shift.

I yelled to him, "Tommy, wait!" I jogged to catch up with him in the hallway.

He looked back at me, "What's up, kid?" he replied.

"Have you heard from Bill? He didn't show up for shift change. I called his house. No answer."

"No, I haven't seen him. He didn't show up for his shift? That's odd..." said Officer Maestas.

I thought to myself that maybe we should go check on him. I asked Tommy "Do you think we could swing by his place? I just want to check on him."

Officer Maestas replied "Yeah, give me ten minutes. We'll go check on him." Maestas patted me on the back like a kid.

"Ok, cool, thanks!" I walked back to my desk mumbling under my breath, "Dick!"

Tommy's head turned back to me, "What's that?"

I thought quickly on my feet and replied, "Nothing... I'm just worried sick." I plopped into my desk chair, staring at the clock, waiting for it to turn 8:15 p.m. My thoughts wandered away from me. The tick of the clock felt like a form of meditation. I was lost in my head.

"Erik..." Tommy's deep voice startled me and I jumped up from my chair. "You ready, bro?" he said.

"Uh, yyyeah! Let me get my shit," I stuttered.

4

Both of us jumped into Tommy's badass Charger and headed toward Bill's house. It was the longest I'd ever been around Maestas. He wasn't the talkative type most of the time and the car was awkwardly quiet. I tried coming up with something to break the silence, but each time the words came to mouth, I shoved back down and shut up. I sat there, nervously looking out the window. I kept wiping my hands back and forth on my pant legs. I tried my hardest to think of something to break the ice. It seemed like Tommy was having one of his days. Word around the office was that Tommy would have his good days and his bad days. He could be nice one day and a total dick the next day. I heard he drank a lot. I could kind of smell it once we got into the car. But I gave him the benefit of the doubt. I snuck his file when he transferred to see what he was about. Boy, I wished I wouldn't have. His file was honestly devastating and disheartening. I'd felt so bad for the guy after reading that his wife and 6 year old son were killed in a car accident the year before. I never brought it up, but it explained a lot. I thought of asking him if he wanted to get a drink to talk about it, but I never did. I just stayed quiet about it. He didn't ever talk about them. Right when I was about to open my mouth to ask him if he wanted to get a drink, the radio went off: "6161, we have multiple complaints of a female screaming. Possible domestic. Please respond." Tommy gasped in relief as he reached for the radio mic. "6161, this is Officer Maestas. I'll take it. I'm on route. Send me the address, we're standing by. Over."

"Sorry kid. Duty calls. We'll go check on Bill after this call," said Tommy, in a frustrated voice, flicking his sirens on. The cop car gained speed as we flew through the intersections. My hands gripped my thighs tighter and tighter, reaching back I pulled the seat belt over my shoulder, clicking it just to be safe. Tommy looked over at me, kind of giving me a dirty look, as I sat nervously. I felt the speed of the car pushing me back against my seat. Tommy took a hard right and we pulled up to the house. The car hit the curb, coming to a dead stop. Tommy quickly grabbed the radio mic calling in, "6161...I just arrived at the scene. Stand by for further information."

Tommy threw the mic to the floor with his game face on. I'd never seen him that serious.

"Whatever happens kid, stay in the car. I don't want to be responsible for your ass getting shot, or something." He looked back at me waiting for reassurance.

"Ok," I softly replied.

"Did you hear me kid? Whatever happens, stay in the car" Tommy reiterated.

"Ok, I got it!" I barked back, knowing that could've been my chance to finally shine. I scowled at the floor, rubbing my legs as anxiety shot through my entire body. Tommy got out of the car, slamming the door behind him. The blue and red lights reflected up and down the block. Tommy placed his right hand on his gun as he reached for the mic attached to his uniform. He walked up the lawn in a cautious manner, onto the porch, his hand placed on the perch of his gun. I sat in the car, quietly watching, as Tommy knocked on the door. I could hear his voice coming through the police scanner. "6161... Officer Maestas on scene. I'm walking up to the house now. Stand by." Then I could faintly hear him as he commanded, "Denver Police, OPEN UP." Officer Maestas waited patiently at the door, not receiving any response. He banged on the screen door one more time, "Denver PD, OPEN UP!" He grabbed the flashlight out of his holster, shining it through the window, walking back and forth. He continued shining it into the windows. I continued to sit there, in anticipation, rubbing my legs like a moron. I leaned over the dashboard to get a better look.

Tommy walked down the stairs, his right hand still on his weapon, his flashlight still in his other hand, as he walked to the right side of the house, shining his flashlight into each window as he passed. He stepped toward the back of the house. The radio was dead silent and I didn't see Officer Maestas anywhere. It was too quiet. I could hear a dog barking from down the street though. My heart raced as

I waited for Tommy to walk back to the front. I started to panic, so I decided to get out of the car. I placed my right hand on my firearm, knowing that if Tommy saw me get out of the car, I would get an ass chewing like no other. Impatiently, I paced outside of the car, weighing my decision. I had to have his back. Something didn't feel right. I urged myself to go in and check. I hadn't shot a gun since the academy, I thought to myself, walking up to the lawn cautiously. My heart began pounding in my chest faster and faster. A nervous sweat dripped down my forehead.

I timidly called out to Officer Maestas, "Tommy...what the Hell's going on?" As I got close enough to look through the front window, I couldn't see Officer Tommy's flashlight, or anything at all for that matter. The inside of the house was too dark to see into the windows. Too much time has passed by without a sign of Tommy or the residents. I took a deep breath, again calling out to see if I could get an answer from Tommy.

"Tommy..."

A gunshot lit up the front room of the house, followed by a flash. POP! I stood there, frozen, my heart shooting down to my stomach. POP POP POP! Three more shots rang out, lighting up the living room windows behind the yellow curtains. I thought to myself in a panic, 'Help his ass, Erik." I pulled my gun out of the holster and sprinted to the back of the house as fast as I could, leaping over the small fence that divided the yard from the driveway. Holding my gun at firing stance, my heart pounded through my bullet proof vest. The back door was wide open. The inside of the house was pitch black.

5

I forcefully whispered out to Tommy, "Tommy, what the fuck?" I reached for my flashlight with my left hand, extending my gun in the other. It was hard to see in the house, my flashlight was a piece of shit, too apparently. Of course I would get the piece of shit flashlight that didn't work when I needed it to. I had to take a deep breath before I hyperventilated. I wiped the sweat away from my face with my sleeve. My breathing went from 0 to 60 in seconds. I slowly and cautiously walked into the back door lightly calling out to Officer Maestas.

"Tommy, where are you? What's your status?" My flashlight in one hand and my 9mm in the other, I cautiously entered the kitchen from the stairs that led from the back door. I received no response from Tommy. I accidentally bumped into the kitchen table on my right, making a grating sound across the tile, scaring the crap out of myself. I turned the light towards the dining room as I entered, firearm drawn. I heard a rustling sound coming from one of the bedrooms. In a panic, I ran through the living room, shining my flashlight, desperately trying not to fall on anything. A creaking sound came from behind my shoulder. I swung my light around, firing off two shots without thinking. An older gentleman sat in his brown rocking chair with two gun holes in his chest and one in his forehead. The back of his head painted the wall behind him. The old man rocked back and forth. Panic gutted me as I thought I had hit the old man. 'Fuck, fuck, fuck….' I said to myself as I ran over to see if he was still alive. As I got closer, I could see the old man's mouth was covered in black bio. The stench of it was overwhelmingly strong; a pungent odor escaped from the body. I had only fired twice, but the body had three rounds in it. As I moved my light around, I noticed that the wall behind the man had two smoking bullet holes. I'd missed when I fired. It discouraged me. It must have been Tommy that had shot the old man.

The house suddenly shook from a loud crash in a room down the hallway. Knocking and rustling continued to come from one of the bedrooms down the hallway.

I called out to Tommy once more, "Tommy! What the hell?"

Out of nowhere, I heard Tommy's muffled voice, "Son of a bitch!" I bolted down the hallway, kicking the door open, flashing my light in the corner of the room, gun ready. I saw Tommy with a young girl on top of him hissing and clawing at him. He was trying to fight her, but his face was smashed to the floor, with her hand pressed against his face. As I reacted, I dropped my flashlight, causing the entire room to go dark. My flashlight rolled and swung around the floor. In the dim light, I ran toward Tommy and his attacker. The light spun in the middle of the room, throwing off my depth perception, making it practically impossible to see what was going on. I placed my gun quickly in its holster as I grabbed the girl from behind by her t-shirt and shoulder. It took a lot more strength than I'd expected. It was as if she'd weighed a ton, with a crazy amount of strength added in. She punched Tommy in the face and his head bounced off the floor with each blow this tiny little girl dished out. She was violently attacking him and then just as quickly, spun around; her tiny fist swung around, busting me in the lip as I attempted to pull her off. My hands released her from my grasp and jumped back onto Tommy, struggling in a fight to the death, or so it seemed. Her punch knocked me back into the dresser. She'd punched me so hard that I was dizzy. The FLASH punch was so quick and unexpected, it had caught me completely off guard. Once I finally regained my composure, I popped my neck back and forth and reached my hands out to pull her off of Tommy. Her arm swung back towards me as she hissed and growled. She let out a shriek that led me to believe that this wasn't just a little girl. She was fighting both of us like she was a fucking psycho on leave from the fuckling nut house. I wondered what drug she'd taken that had given her such super strength. I plunged my right hand into the back of her neck and grabbed her by her hair, finally pulling her off and throwing her into the corner of the room. Her head put a hole into the wall as Tommy grabbed the dresser next to him trying to stand and regain his breath; coughing from her choke hold. As quick as she went down, she popped right up, springing up to her feet. Her arms hung like a primitive ape in the middle of a battle for domination. She slammed her fist on the ground as her anger grew. eyes seemed to be infused with blood, but it was hard to see in the dim light. They darted back and forth aggressively. I tried to calm her down, placing my hands in a defensive position. Tommy spit the blood from his mouth and wiped away the blood on his face, as I attempted to take control of the situation. Both of us backed into a corner of the room shouting out at the girl.

"You need to calm down, miss." The sound of my voice froze her in mid pace, like it caught her attention. She slowly twisted her body over to us. Tommy whispered out, " I thought I told you to stay in the car, kid…" I glared at him, not that he could see in the darkness. Confidently, Tommy whispered again "I had everything under control." Despite the seriousness of the moment, I had to giggle a little bit.

"Yeah? You had getting your ass beat by a little girl totally under control." The little girl growled in the corner catching both of our attention once again. It was starting to scare me a little bit how crazy this girl was acting. It looked like she had rabies. She was angry and foaming blood from her mouth. Black bio goo dripped down onto her feet. She stood in the corner, her hair covering her face, as the blood soaked the carpet. She hissed and moaned through her teeth. The flashlight illuminated half of her body and the right corner of the room

"Miss! Back the fuck off, or I'll be forced to fire!"

Tommy slapped my arm, putting both hands up in the air, questioning my statement.

"What?" I was confused.

Tommy whispered over to me, "You don't tell a little girl that. What the hell's the matter with you?" We argued back and forth in a whisper.

"I'm not actually gonna shoot her, you know. I'm just trying to take control of the situation."

Tommy whispered through gritted teeth, "What the hell's the matter with you, you idiot?"

Her foot slid slowly across the rug. I panicked again and pulled my gun out. Tommy yelled at me, "Don't Shoot her Erik!" He reached over and pulled my shoulder, yelling out to the little girl, "STAY BACK. STAY WHERE YOU ARE! You need to stay back!"

The little girl shuffled her feet towards us, hissing through her teeth. Without hesitation, the little girl screamed at the top of her lungs, lunging at us both. I closed one eye and squeezed the trigger. POP, POP, POP! Shots lit up the dark room briefly. One popped her in the shoulder, another in her cheek, the last one whistled right between her eyes. The back of her head painted the wall behind her as she fell over into the corner lifeless. Scared shitless, I had shouted at the top of my lungs, "What the hell?" Tommy continued to catch his breath as he'd lowered his weapon. My three shots smoked in the ceiling of the room (2 feet away from the girl's body). Tommy's shot had taken her down. He was covered in his own blood, and her bio, from the ass beating he'd taken. Blood painted the room, covering the walls and soaking the carpet. I'd never seen anything like it before. The smell that came from the room, the blood stench and rot, was all consuming. Tommy wiped the blood on his face with his left arm as he holstered his weapon. He gave a look that told me not to say a word.

He grabbed his mic with his hand. "I'm going to radio this in," he said as he walked away, his eyes glued to the floor in disappointment.

I stood there, in shock at what the hell had happened. I walked over to grab my flashlight. As I bent over to pick it up, I stared at the young lady, laying there, covered in blood. I took in a deep breath and pulled the bed sheet off the bed to cover the body. The white sheet instantly absorbed her blood. As I walked down the hallway, I stopped in to review what had happened with the old man. He had two bite marks on his forearm that I hadn't noticed before. The bite marks had obviously come from the little girl, but why the hell would she bite him? What would cause a little girl to lose her mind and attack everyone? What could have given such anger and immense strength? I walked out the front door and stood at the porch as Tommy walked to the car, not saying a word. He also looked confused about the whole situation. I stood there on the porch, shaking a little and trying to pace my breathing. Tommy grabbed his radio, "6161...We have two bodies on the scene. Requesting clean up and medical attention, 11-41, code 10-26, all clear, 10-4."

Tommy bit his lip as he lowered his radio. Sirens wailed through the neighborhood to join us. I stood by the car, speechless. Neither of us spoke. The ambulance sped around the corner quickly. Two more cop cars pulled up behind the ambulance. All the lights made the neighborhood look like a carnival. Officer Maestas walked away from the car as he met up with the other officers. All three of them grabbed for their flashlights as they walked up the lawn. One of them shined their light into my face. The glare of his light instantly pissed me off. I blocked the light from my face and watched them all walk through the front door. No one said a word. I stood by the car and watched an officer grab the police tape and tape the front yard off as all the neighbors gathered around to gossip. Tommy emerged from the house and walked back to his car. I heard him tell one of the other uniforms, "Take Officer McAllister home. He's seen enough." He glanced at me with a serious look on his face. I put my hands in the air in the most exaggerated what the fuck motion possible. Bill, one of the officers, walked up to me, grabbed me by the arm and grumbled, "Come on, McAllister, let's go. You heard him." I was pissed. I had practically saved his life and he was kicking me to the curb. They didn't even ask me what had happened. I stood firmly rooted on the porch with my hands on my hips. Bill yelled out to me, "McAllister! LET'S GO!"

CHAPTER 4

Officer McAllister

A couple hours had gone by after the incident during the disturbance call. Bill had brought me back to the station and I walked home. That night, everything played through my mind. over and over. I had never seen anything like that. I had so many questions. The look on that girl's fucked up face had scared the shit out of me. What reason would Tommy need to shoot an old man in a rocking chair, not once, but three times? The whole situation was odd. Neither of them had even had weapons, but she had been immensely strong. Had the old man been that way, too? I had laid on my bed, staring at the ceiling. I hated being stuck at home, staring at the walls, but my mind was so boggled.

    I always kept my police scanner next to my bed to keep up with everything. The radio went all night. There seemed to have been a lot of domestic violence calls; more than I'd ever heard. People were being attacked left and right. Calls constantly buzzed through the radio. My mind wandered with curiosity about everything that had, and continued to, happen. I climbed out of bed, wiping the nervous sweat from my brow; exhausted from being deep in thought for hours. My eyes glanced and the clock as I took a deep breath and walked over to the TV. I figured that there was nothing more mind numbing than late night infomercials. I changed the channel to the news to see if anything was broadcasting about the rise in domestic calls. I needed to find something to make sense of the events that had happened earlier today. Tommy had to have known more than he had told me. Nothing was even said about the old man, or the little girl, that two police officers had shot without reason. Not a word. It was like a fucking cover up. Guilt clenched at my gut.

2

Something wasn't right. My instincts screamed at me that something big was going on and I needed to know what it was. My mind searched desperately for explanation. It was a deep pit in the middle of my stomach that needed to be filled. I planned to do everything that I could to find out. The radio was wild; one right after another the calls rolled through dispatch. One of the calls caught my attention; a police officer called in distress. I cranked the radio volume up.

"760- We have a police officer down!"

The operator on the radio responded, "Was the officer shot? I need to know what happened."

The police officer screamed through the radio, responding aggressively. I slid over in bed, practically pressing my ear to the speaker. The officer shouted, "I don't know what happened. I turned around and some girl bit him on his neck. There's blood everywhere." The officer spoke desperately to the downed officer in the background, "Stay with me! Stay with me! Help will be here any second now. I need you to hold on."

The officer on the radio screamed into his mic forcefully again, "GET SOMEONE THE FUCK OUT HERE NOW! HE'S DYING!"

My heart was pounding with empathy and devastation, helplessness; knowing that I couldn't do a thing to help. The dispatcher responded back to the police officer, "Someone is on the way. Keep pressure on the wound. I need you to stay calm!" Another influx of calls flooded the radio.

3

The TV broadcasts on every channel reported that the world was going crazy; Hell on earth they said. Every station led with the headline: "A VIRUS OUTBREAK IS TAKING OVER THE WORLD". The entire world spiraled in a free fall of impending doom. Reporters on the news stood in front of the White House reporting with the military surrounding them.

A young reporter's voice trembled in fear, "The dead are walking the earth and eating the flesh of the living." Gunshots shot out in the background; rapid gunfire which drowned out the reporter's already meak voice. The reporter was trying to keep her composure and be as professional as she could, but her awareness of the chaos unfolding was obvious. One of the infected tackled the cameraman to the ground; leaving the footage to show every flip and roll of the dropped camera before it was picked back up. The camera man and the reporter ran for their very lives up the lawn of the white house. The infected followed them without hesitation. The reporter ran up the stairs of the white house pounding on the front door.

The camera swung back and forth, capturing the gruesome image of the military fighting the hoards of infected that swarmed the front lawn of the white house. They flooded over the gate, climbing over one another. The military personnel retreated back in a shootout against the dead. The infected chased each one of them down, tearing them to pieces and moving on to the next. It was nearly impossible to believe that what I was seeing was real. Before the reporter and the cameraman could even get past the doors of the white house, they were overcome by a flood of infected who worked to rip them apart. One of the dead headbutted the reporter, forcing her to fall to the ground unconscious. The cameraman swung the camera over to meet the face of one of the infected, dropping the infected to the ground. He rapidly slammed the camera into the head of the infected over and over until the lens of the camera was covered in the blood and brains of the infected man. The camera shook violently and the news station cut the feed back to the anchor. She didn't even speak; her face pale and covered in pure shock. The voice of her producer whispered out to her, telling her that she had to say something. She just sat there frozen, clearing her throat, adjusting the papers on her desk.

Finally a string of stuttered words came together in the right way. "I apologize for that graphic footage. On behalf of the members at CNC, we pray for the members of the media out amid the chaos." Her voice sounded scripted.

I couldn't believe what I'd witnessed. It was just like in the movies; people were dropping like flies, then coming back to life in the matter of seconds. The dead chased people around and devoured them like rabid animals. My logical mind refused to believe that some virus was consuming the living and then using their bodies as hosts. It wasn't fucking possible. The news broadcast anchor forced herself to mutter words again, "If you are just joining us, I'm Anabelle Poe. With me, is my co-anchor, Nick Mozee. Reports around the world are flooding in. It appears that a virus, or disease, has taken the world by storm. Hundreds to thousands are reported to be infected. If you come into contact with an individual who appears to have come in contact with the virus, get away from them as soon as you can. Find a safe place to hide, do not leave your house, lock, and barricade if possible, all your doors and windows. Military personnel are working to assist you and your families. We go now to Jeff Hammack, live at the CDC in New York. Jeff."

There was a long pause as Jeff stared into the camera with a pensive look on his face. "Thank you, Anabelle. We have spoken to CDC officials. They are going to have a press conference moments from now. We are waiting for word, as we stand by."

An official from the CDC stepped up to the podium. His eyes looked bloodshot and tired, the sweat on his brow thick and glistening. He cleared his throat, "Before I get started, my name is Victor Kate. I'm a specialist in disease control and Superintendent of the CDC. The virus that has taken the world by storm is nothing that we at the CDC have ever seen before."

He took a deep, lingering breath, but just before he could get another word out, muffled gunshots began popping off in the background. Distant screams echoed in chaos and the camera moved over to the view of two white double doors. Everyone in the room had their attention fixated on the doors as gunshots sounded off directly behind the doors. Both doors burst open and a flood of infected rushed in; some lunged at the people sitting in the chairs. Suddenly the room was a feeding frenzy. The infected rushed the camera; screams filled the room...agony. A free for all commenced as blood rained in the room. Panic took the room by storm. The feed to the camera cut to the standby screen.

4

The news anchor, Anabelle Poe, popped back up on the screen in tears, trying her best to keep it together. The tape down at the bottom of the screen scrolled: PLEASE STAY CALM AND REMAIN IN YOUR HOMES. Clearing her throat as she attempted to choke back her tears, Miss Poe spoke, "Nobody knows, or can say what this virus is, or what is causing it to spread so rapidly. They are unsure of where it is in orientation." Anabelle Poe, having little information, remained tearful, but professional.

"The CDC has reported they've never seen a virus that moves at such a rapid pace, nor one that has demonstrated such aggressive and violent symptoms. The CDC has stated that there is no telling where it originated from. It broke out in eastern countries and rapidly hit the western part of the world; consuming everything in its path. People are crying out in mass hysteria for their governments to do something, riots are ensuing around the world. Panic has consumed the people all around the world." The anchor's voice broke as she wiped tears from her face. "The President of The United States has yet to be found. Reports from government officials say they've yet to locate the President. He was last seen getting on Air Force One; they have lost contact with Air Force One, so they are unsure of his whereabouts, or if he has gone safely into hiding. On the eastern side of the United States in cities such as New York and Boston, reports of extreme rioting and looting are coming through."

I sat there at the edge of my bed, my eyes glued to the television, turning up the volume as high as it could go. "Police officials out of New York are reporting that they have lost containment and the National Guard is in retreat. It is not safe to be out in the streets of New York or New Jersey. The George Washington bridge has fallen. Airliners are failing to reach their destinations. Moments ago, United Airlines flight 787, flying out of JFK Airport, crashed into the Hudson River. The right wing of the plane took out the middle of the

George Washington bridge, killing hundreds. The remainder of the bridge buckled from the weight of everyone trying to escape the city. People are stranded on either side of the bridge, with nowhere to go. There is no telling how many total are dead. It hasn't been longer than 24 hours since the first reports of the outbreak began, but California up to Seattle and down to Mexico are seeing signs of the virus. The reports seem to show that in the matter of 13 hours, the virus has spread rapidly throughout, not only the United States, but also the world. Folks, this is unprecedented."

I wiped my sweaty hands across my face. My eyes were dried out. I don't think that I had blinked throughout the entire report.

"Hollywood Hills has erupted in flames. The entire city is in pure chaos. The Los Angeles tri state area has erupted in rioting and looting, making it impossible to tell who is infected with the virus. The government has closed the city off. There is no one allowed to enter or exit the tri state area."

The news was reporting that major celebrities, such as Arnold Schwarzenegger, had opted to stay and help government officials regain control of the city. All police and firefighters were called upon for active duty.

"Again, if you are just joining us, I'm Anabelle Poe and with me is Nick Mozee. Anyone who comes in contact with the infected please be advised that transfer appears to occur via scratch, bite, or any type of blood or saliva transfer. Infection appears to occur in a matter of a few minutes for most and in a few rare examples, hours. The primary cause of transfer is a bite. If infected, the individual becomes deceased, then seems to come back to life, showing homicidal aggression. The disease, or virus, is causing the infected to become violent, with uncontrollable rage and aggression. It mimics rabies, except that it kills you prior to you exhibiting any symptoms. People are attacking each other like severely starved wild animals."

The anchors sent the report out to another young reporter in Time Square. She pointed behind her as one of the rioters in the background fell backwards against the wall, arching his neck away from the infected that attacked him. Like a beast, it stretched its neck and plunged its teeth into the neck of its victim. It clenched down on a chunk of flesh from that man's neck, pulling it away. The flesh showed some kind of resistance. The veins in the victim's neck exploded with the force. Blood erupted and painted the face of the infected man. The victim screamed in pain until blood flooded from his mouth, altering his screams into gurgles. The entire attack, every sight and sound, was shown on live TV. The brutality of it was maddening to watch. No one around even tried to help him...no one was trying to help anyone else in fact. Even the reporter and the cameraman just stood there gawking. The victim's blood curdling scream was ear piercing and grabbed the attention of more of the infected. One right after another descended upon the victim. The reporter watched in pure shock while the camera captured that man being ripped apart like it was nothing. He laid there, screaming in agony, for someone to help him. The camera seemed to capture something else. One of the infected appeared to have noticed the reporter standing there. The light of the camera beamed on the attack group. The infected ran toward the reporter, plowing into both her and the cameraman.

The camera quickly lost focus; the sound of her voice faded in and out as the cameraman fumbled to regain control. I can't say how, but they were both able to get back to their feet. The infected man chased them, forcing both of them to run for their lives. The reporter tried to regain her breath. She launched her heels off and took off even faster. The infected man lost focus on the reporter and cameraman as he passed another looter by a store front; dodged to the left and tackled the man through the doorway of the store. The reporter and the cameraman looked back. The reporter attempted to catch her breath, still trying to give the report while chaos emerged in the background; virtually impossible to differentiate between infected and the civilians. Both the cameraman and the reporter dodged left and right, desperately trying to avoid their numerous attackers. The female reporter attempted to yell over the crowd noise and chaos. I had to commend her for attempting to keep doing her job while monsters were trying to tear her to shreds. "Mass hysteria has broken out in the middle of downtown New York and the infected are running through the streets of Time Square. Rioting and looting are making it impossible to tell who is infected and who is a civilian. I've never witnessed anything like it. OH MY GOD! HERE THEY COME! RUN, RICKY!"

The reporter and the cameraman paused, looked around, and immediately noticed the crowd of infected which surrounded them. It was hopeless. Police were forced to shoot anything that moved; shooting civilians and the infected. Swat teams had barricaded Time Square in an attempt to protect any of the civilians as best they could, but any civilians trying to seek quick shelter were being targeted as infected victims. I sat there glued to the TV with both hands on top of my head, pinning my sweaty hair back and staring at the TV in amazement, watching the apocalypse unfold. The cameraman was running as fast as he could, carrying that heavy ass camera; the reporter reported in broken sentences. One of the infected jumped on top of her, tackling her to the ground and bumping the cameraman to the ground in the process. The camera man lost grip of his camera; it smashed onto the ground and landed facing the reporter. She began screaming for her dear life; gut wrenching, horrified shrieks. Her screams echoed throughout my apartment. My heart pounded through my chest. I swallowed back vomit. Watching that woman get attacked on live TV had to have terrified every home in the nation. Watching her brutal murder unfold on live television left me speechless; in shock. Ten or so of the infected jumped on top of her, attacking her violently, biting and clawing at her, one of them pulling her by her hair, slamming her head against the ground in a rage I had never seen before. Her beautiful face was crushed repeatedly into the sidewalk until she was unrecognizable.

Her head hit the ground so hard you could hear the crunching of her skull each time. Blood began squirting out of her eyes and mouth coating the lens of the camera. The woman's screams were but faint grains. It sent chills down my spine. The cameraman scooped up his camera, with it still facing the reporter, and ran away from the infected that attacked his colleague. Most of the infected continued to rip her to pieces, but some of the infected branched off to chase after the cameraman. His camera continued to roll and suddenly the dead reporter quickly leapt to her feet; her face completely mangled, her cheek hanging off of her face as she began puking blood and running at the cameraman. All I could hear was the cameraman's breathing and screams of chaos around him. New York had fallen. The signal of the cameraman in Time Square was lost and a stand by signal covered every screen in Los Angeles briefly. When the two news anchors reappeared on my screen, they didn't speak. There were tears in both of their eyes and they just sat there, staring into the camera.

5

Nick Mozee picked up the papers in front of him on the desk, stacking them neatly in front of him. He swallowed deeply, clearing his throat, nervously loosening his tie. Not a word came out of his mouth. He was sweaty. You could see the sweat dripping off his nose. Leaning over to the female anchor, Anabelle Poe, he tried to whisper in her ear, but her mic picked it up.

"People out there are dropping like flies. How much longer do we have to do this?"

The station switched over to a reporter in Los Angeles. I stood there and realized that I hadn't breathed. I gasped for air, dizzy. I tried to quell my nervousness. I walked over to the bathroom mirror, flicking the light on. The room began to spin. My throat felt tight. My nerves came up and out so fast that I missed the toilet. I threw up all over the side of the bathtub, catching myself on the seat of the toilet. My stomach squeezed tighter and tighter, but all I could throw up was yellow acid. I couldn't catch my breath and I began to hyperventilate. Honestly, I felt like crying, but I tried my best to keep it together. I pulled my weakened body up to the sink, turning on the cold water. Instantly the coolness of the water relieved me of my nausea. Sipping the cool water rid the stench of puke out of my mouth. I stared deeply into my own eyes, attempting to find myself, attempting to find some courageous way to respond to the world coming

6

I shook my head in dismay as I wiped the water from my face onto my shirt. Anxiety pumped furiously through my body. I was shaking, terrified to my very core. I had no idea what to do. My glance landed on the bullet proof vest hanging on my kitchen chair. My ego reared up again and I figured that was my final chance to ever shine. I suited up, strapped into my vest and grabbed my gun from the kitchen table. Then, I grabbed the bottle of whiskey out of the bottom cabinet, twisted the cap off and slammed the rest of the bottle. I squeezed the top of the chair, trying to gain some amount of courage, looking down at my feet and mulling over what I could do. Officer Maestas. If he was still alive, he would know what to do. I paused at the door, hesitant to leave the safety of my home. I had to force myself to stop being a pussy. I had sworn to serve and protect. My time had come. I somehow knew that once I walked through that door, I wouldn't be coming back. The building was far more quiet than ever; not a peep came out of any of the apartments. Usually Mrs. Pedman had her TV immensely loud and you could hear her stupid ass dog barking, but it was dead quiet. The sound of the light bulbs buzzing and flickering was a little too eerie for me. SI felt the need to knock and check on her. Fuck. I chuckled as I thought to myself that the scenario was exactly how people died in horror movies. While I stood there, I heard a shuffling behind the door and a shadow began to move back and forth underneath the door. I stood there with my hand placed on the handle of my gun, thinking I could just shoot the door and end it from right there in the hallway. My conscience got the better of me. What if she was alive and needed help? The shadow inched closer to the door. I timidly moved closer to the door, trying to determine if Mrs. Pedman was alive, or if she was infected. With my ear to the door, I could hear a faint breath, then a hiss, and then a deep cough. A loud thump pounded on the back of the door, catching me off guard and forcing me to jump back. My 9mm was pulled out, ready to fire. I holstered it and decided to run as fast as I could to the station and find Maestas. I took off down the hallway, my eyes saw shadows moving back and forth under all of the doorways.

Once I was outside, I gasped for air, breathing deeply once again. It was dead silent outside, too. It was starting to freak me out. It's one thing to see it on the TV, but another to see it happening around you. I looked up to Mrs. Pedman's window. Through her sheer, white drapes, I saw the figure of a tiny woman. It was the scariest shit. She had no movement, her face blank, a shadow peering through the drapes. The light in the window flashed on and off before the window went dark and made the figure in the window disappear. Tommy. I needed to find Tommy. I turned away and ran. I didn't stop.

CHAPTER 5

Officer Tommy Maestas

"Death Is Not The Greatest Of Evils, It Is Worse To Want To Die, And Not Be Able To"...the quote, by Sophocles, was one of the greatest quotes I had ever heard...until it brought truth to my life. It didn't matter what I did. I couldn't escape from the haunting, painful past. Each dawning day I woke up to the dark abyss of my loneliness, in my empty room, and carried it to the moment my eyes closed at night. Even then, the nightmares crushed me until I woke up screaming, in a cold sweat. Thoughts of my wife Jenny, and my son Carson's, deaths haunted me every moment. My heart held them so dearly and I honestly was sure I would never move on. Everything I did from the moment of their deaths reminded me of them: a certain smell, or something of Jenny's that was left behind... it all kept me anchored in this perpetual nightmare. Carson's room was still the way he'd left it the day they had left the house and never returned. Sometimes I would go into his room, lay in his bed and squeeze the shit out of his favorite stuffed teddy bear. It would never fail to bring me to pieces. I'll admit it! I would burst into tears every time, unable to control myself. It'd been almost a year and I could still smell him on his sheets. The smell of his shampoo entrapped into his pillow... Johnson's baby shampoo. Not a day went by where I didn't attempt to drink myself to death to ease the regret that I couldn't save them. I should have done something different.

    I was to be forever pained, forced to suffer; eternally reliving the moment in my head. Paini was an understatement, to say the least. Some days I sat in his room for hours just thinking- holding that damn bear tightly in my arms; as if it were Carson himself. I'd lay there holding it, until the pain became too much and I could hold it no more. It was like holding your hand onto a hot burner till the pain forced you to blackout. Each day that I woke up, I stared at the clock, watching it change minute by minute. I rolled over to find nothing but an empty space; nothing but the indent of Jenny, an ever present reminder of my loss and grief. Most mornings, I woke up sliding my hand across the bed hoping Jenny was there...praying that it had been a nightmare. I could almost feel her there some mornings, but then realized it was just the vast emptiness fooling me. I know it was probably disgusting, but I couldn't bring myself to wash the smell of her out of the sheets. I could still smell her as if she'd been there all along. She always got out of the shower and came to bed to lay down; her body wet and naked, the bed sheets soaking up the smell of her freshness. The moment that she was next to me, I would hold her; if only just to feel my fingertips slide across her smooth skin. I would find any excuse to pull her close to me; always brushing her thick, long, black hair through my fingers away from her face. When she went to bed, I had to get up for my shift, but nothing could pull me away from her. Nothing could release her from my grip. But then, every night, there I was staring at the ceiling, alone. It felt like someone was constantly kicking me in the chest, coupled with the splitting headache from my attempts to drown myself in bottles of scotch or whiskey.

    I'd sit up in bed and ask myself everyday: why? Why do I let myself suffer? I wanted to...needed to...die. Every day. I should've just ended it; killed myself and gotten it over with, but I was too much of a pussy to pull the trigger. More than once I had shoved the gun into the bottom of my chin, crying to the point I couldn't breathe and screaming at the top of my lungs. My heart was shattered and I didn't know how to fix it. The thought ran through my mind all day, every day. It wasn't a matter of how, but when I would kill myself. Plenty of times I'd sat in my chair, in the dark, with a bottle of scotch or whiskey, twirling my 9mm bullet through my fingers, placing it in the chamber and putting the gun in my mouth. I'd even grabbed my belt and looped it through the buckle, put a knot at the end and shoved it between the top of the door, wedging it, and standing on a chair. All I had to do was kick the chair from under me. I never could go through with it. The one time I did, it broke; the weight of my body plunged to the ground. I drove around in my squad car and thought about how I would do it; what would be the most painless way to do it. Maybe I would just crash my car into an oncoming car, or swerve my car off a bridge. Coming home to an empty house after work each day, a house that was dead quiet, just reminded me of how much I missed them. I missed them!!! So much; to the point that my soul was hollow. The pain slowly killed it; shattering it like broken glass. Masking the pain with alcohol didn't do a damn thing.

2

Sometimes I went to the same bar where I met Jenny when she was in college. She was there with her college buddies. It was practically impossible to talk to her back then. She had all her college football buddies huddled around her, like they were her 300 pound body guards. I'd waited until the time was right to sneak in and say, "Hi." It took forever, but I'd finally found the courage to go and talk to her. After coming straight out of the police academy, I thought I was pretty badass. Those dudes looked at me like they wanted to beat my ass. One of the football players immediately jumped in my face asking me if I was lost. I can't remember what I said, but he punched the shit out of me, causing a big brawl in the bar and getting us all arrested. But, I guess I must've been charming enough for her to remember me the next time she was in there. I eventually married Jenny. The day I met her, I was instantly in love. There wasn't any way I wasn't bringing her home with me forever. Soon we'd had our son, Carson, filling an empty house with so much happiness and laughter. God, I loved them so much. But all I'd had since they'd died was a house filled with the damn sound of the TV, and decorated with empty liquor bottles everywhere. Everyone said that with time the pain would go away, but that was not true. With time, I learned to shroud my pain from the outside world, to function somewhat, but my pain never, ever went away. It became more intense with each day that passed. After Jenny and Carson were killed in the accident, I fell apart. I quit everything but my job. I took a leave of absence till I was ready to go back, but I couldn't stay at home. It was killing me slowly and very painfully.

3

I would never forget that day. I remembered the call on my radio word for word: "634- an accident has been reported on Route 6, westbound. Witnesses say there's a female and a small child involved and in need of medical assistance. Please respond." I was driving back to the station that day from a noise complaint over on 38th. At first I hadn't put the pieces of the puzzle together because I had just gotten off the phone with my wife Jenny, not even five minutes before the call came through dispatch. They were coming back from her parent's lake house. Every year they would get together at the lake house to spend the week together. I hated going. Every year I dreaded going, but somehow Jenny would convince me to go.

"It's not that bad," she would say. She had a heart of gold, but she could manipulate me to get what she wanted. I'd decided to stay that time. I hadn't given her the time of day to try to work her magic on me. I'd told her firmly that I was staying for work. Every year it was the same bullshit with her family. I did everything in my power to get out of going to her parent's lake house so I didn't have to hear her brother's lame ass stories of how he'd saved a damn seal off the coast, or how he'd saved the lives of whales from poacher's by protesting on a damn fishing boat. I just never gave a shit about that kind of shit. Listening to her father complain that everything I did was good enough. Being a cop was too dangerous for my family and I should've worked for him selling cars. I'd almost punched his ass a couple times. The guy could really get under my skin quite easily. Jenny had begged me and begged me to go to the lake for the week. I'd kept telling her that I had to work and I couldn't get the time off because of a case I was working.

4

I remembered that I was walking up the stairs at the station and something told me to give Jenny a call, so I had stopped to call her, just to be safe. The phone had just rang and rang, and then gone to voicemail. I'd called her twice before running back to my squad car, my heart pounding in my chest. I didn't know why I felt so concerned. I jumped into my car and sped out of the parking lot like a bat out of hell. I'd kept calling and calling...it would just go straight to her voice When my phone rang, it had caused me to jump. Thinking it was Jenny, I had promptly answered the call. It was my friend, and colleague, Officer Miller, telling me to get to Route 6 as soon as I could; that Jenny and Carson had been in an accident. My worst nightmare had come to life. I'd driven as fast as I could; swerving in and out of lanes, passing cars, throwing my sirens on, forcing cars to get the hell out of my way as I sped down the road. I had lost myself in deep thought: hoping, pleading that they were ok, my heart was beating through my chest from fear of the worst. I was driving so fast that I had almost missed the on ramp to Route 6. My hands had squeezed the steering wheel tighter and tighter until my fingers no longer had any circulation.

I had thought the pounding in my chest might kill me before I arrived at the scene. The more my mind filled in blanks, the worse it had gotten. The longer I was in the squad car, the more unbearable my thoughts became. Traffic blocked the entire highway, making it practically impossible for me to get there. Officer Gary Miller met me as he'd placed flares out on the road. At that moment, I had known that something was very wrong, but I held on to the hope that it wasn't Carson and Jenny. Another officer stood, waving his arms in the middle of the road, flares lit up his neon police vest. The ambulance and fire department were standing around the crash. I had practically run from the car while it was still rolling. My breathing got heavier and tears flooded my eyes.

Gary had stopped me in my tracks. "Tommy, I'm sorry man. I don't know how much longer she has. We are doing everything we can to help." He'd placed his right hand on my shoulder, but I had wiped it away with my hand aggressively. Miller pulled back. I began running as fast as I could to the accident. The smoke had slowly cleared. It was Jenny's jeep. A semi-truck had lost control, swerved into their lane, crushing the whole front of the jeep, pinning Jenny underneath the truck, crushing her from her chest down. The fire department had already cut the door off. Jenny's arm had hung outside of the car, shattered cell phone in hand. She laid there, choking on her own blood. A stream of blood ran down from her mouth to her chin. She had seemed completely unaware of what was going on; though she'd gasped for every breath. The front truck tire smashed the hood of the jeep and blasted the steering wheel into her chest. Her rib cage was crushed. She was fighting for every breath, but had still managed to mutter softly, "Where's Tommy?".

The air to her brain was almost completely cut off. She was hallucinating. My wife had asked me where I was while I stood right next to her, and my heart just shattered.

I had attempted to reassure her, choking, "I'm right here sweetheart. I'm right here."

In a panic, I think that I had scanned the car, desperate to find a way to get her out. Fear gripped me again as I had desperately searched for Carson. He was nowhere to be found. His car seat sat empty. I'd shoved the fire fighters out of my way, grabbed Jenny's phone from her hand, pried it from her grip and thrown it to the ground. I had held her hand, squeezing it as tightly as I could. It had been freezing cold. I had rubbed it against my cheek, knowing in every cell of my body that it was the last time I was going to feel her touch. I had gently stroked her hair, while a river of tears poured from my face.

I tried to look into her eyes. "It's going to be ok, sweetheart. Everything is fine." I repeated myself over and over. More than anything else, I think I was trying to convince myself. That was how I had spent my wife's last seconds on earth. It had felt like an eternity and like I was at warp speed at the same time. I stumbled over my words. I had held her as tightly as I could as she gasped for her last breath.

It sounded like she was going to say something and it never came out. "Where... is....Tommy?..." Those had been her last words. Jenny hadn't even known that I was there. Millions of emotions overcame me at that second; flooding through all at once. I didn't know what to feel. I hadn't known what to do with myself. Freaking out, I'd kissed her cold, lifeless hand and then dropped it to find Carson. They had pulled him from the car before I even arrived.

I couldn't help myself from screaming at the top of my lungs, "Carson where are you?!" I'd waited, hopefully, for Carson's small, sweet voice to let me know he was ok.

One of the firemen had grabbed my shoulder, pointing me to the ambulance. There he was through the doors of the ambulance. He was laying in the ambulance while the medics did everything they could for him. As I walked up to the ambulance, I had frozen in shock, unable to speak; the heart monitor blared, stuck at a steady flat line.

Both medics looked at each other, one of them saying to the other "I'm calling it. Time of death is 5:16 pm". He flopped his body back against the wall. My head felt like it was going to explode. I'd never felt that amount of pain, anger, and heartache all at once. I had shakily climbed my way into the ambulance, reaching for Carson, pulling him by his shirt into my chest. I had taken him into my arms, wrapping both of them under his tiny body and crying hysterically. I held him to my chest as tightly as I could muttering, "Carson? Carson?"... praying he would just wake up and say "I'm fine, daddy!" I repeated his name to myself, over and over, incapable of stopping.

It'd been almost a year and nothing could take away the pain and sorrow. I constantly felt sorry for myself. It felt right to punish myself by providing a slow death due to drinking.

5

The day after all the crap that happened with me and McAllister at that house I had so many questions; so much confusion about the situation. When I had reported back to the police station, they pulled me into the interrogation room with the chief and what looked to be some type of government official. Those assholes told me it had all been taken care of and to keep my mouth shut. In true government dickwad fashion, they had promised to take care of me, as well, if I failed to keep my mouth shut. The guy didn't say a word while we were in the room. He had the chief say it like he was reading a script.

More and more of the same type of incidents were coming on the news. I pulled up to the police station, hungover as fuck. I felt like shit; more so than other days. Feeling like crap was soon to be the last of my worries. Whiskey didn't agree with me as well as the scotch did. I tried to chug my coffee, but it instantly came back up, spraying the left door panel of my door before I could get the son of a bitch open. I knew it was going to be a rough day before I even walked into the station. The station was going crazy, the phones were ringing off the hook, police officers ran in and out. It was pure chaos. I was in a fog. All of the TVs were on, broadcasting the riots and the crazy disturbances occurring downtown. Reports said it was happening all over the world. Fuck, I was foggy. I was lost in thought, sipping what little coffee I had left, walking to my desk. As I passed by the Chief's office, I noticed he had a new look on his face; a look I'd never thought I would see on that man. It was the look of defeat; of exhaustion.

No expression or words were exchanged at that moment. We made eye contact and little did I know that would be the last time we would ever see one another. I shook my head as I gazed on the large stack of paperwork that I had to do. It figured that even during the chaos, the bullshit work continued. I dreaded the long day of typing up reports, hoping that I could avoid taking my files downstairs to Officer McAllister. I tried to take my sweet ass time, but somehow I got done faster than I'd anticipated. As soon as I got downstairs, Officer McAllister gave me the 'let's talk about it' look. What the hell was I supposed to say? Was I supposed to be everyone's damn protector? It was just an awkward silence. I had no words and he had no words. It was bugging the shit out of me. He looked at me like I'd killed his damn puppy, or like I needed to seek revenge against those who had. I was too foggy to care.

In my irritated state I ended up just yelling at him. "What Erik? What was I supposed to do? What the fuck do you want to say? The world is going to shit, so what?"

Erik wiped his hand through his hair, shaking his head, sitting there at his desk and quietly shrugging his shoulders. He looked like a scared little boy, seeking the help of his father. It made me angry. I shoved my finger into his face, biting my lip and shaking my head, but nothing came out. I had nothing to say as I walked away, slamming my hand on the wall. I had no words.

I asked myself over and over what happened on the call with McAllister. What the hell was going on in the damn forsaken world? It seemed like it was burned in my mind and yet the world around me was burning as well. I knew there was something wrong with that girl and her grandfather, but what was wrong with her was a question that the local news sources had answered before I could. All cars were called out to aid in controlling the chaos. My radio mic began going off like crazy. I felt really out of the loop. "787- possible domestic reported, be advised. Be on the lookout for a suspect, white male, short and heavy set. Blue jeans, white shirt, maybe wearing a sports cap. Witnesses say he attacked a male hispanic. Location on the corner Colfax ave. and Perry st. at the 7-11. Witnesses reported one gentleman biting the other male on the hand. Any officers in the area please respond."

6

My mind was heavy as I looked over to my right and saw Officer Gary Miller and his partner, Officer Amanda Stanley, jumping into their squad car speeding off out of the parking lot. Another call going off on the radio "459- burglary in process, two suspects: one male, may be armed and dangerous, proceed with caution." My mind was spinning. The government official, the news had mentioned something about an infection, millions of distress calls bombarded the airwaves; something was definitely wrong. I didn't pay attention to the news very closely...I guess I should have. I couldn't shake from mind the look that the girl and her father had had on their faces, and how they'd attacked me like wild animals. It was imprinted in my mind. I couldn't get it out of my head as I climbed my way into the car, almost forgetting about my cup of coffee, putting the key in the ignition. The car hesitated to start, so I flipped the key again, the car finally turned over. I sat in my squad car just staring at the key swinging back and forth in the ignition, just flat out puzzled. The calls sounded strange. I was so lost in thought that I didn't notice the police officer behind my car. I almost hit him before slamming my foot on the brakes. The police officer slammed his fist on the trunk of the car screaming out, "What the hell man?" and walked to the driver side of the car knocking on the window. It was my friend Officer Higgins. Taking a deep breath, I rolled down the window, "Sorry man! I wasn't paying attention. My bad, bro!"

Officer Higgins looked at me with a frustrated and irritable look on his face and muttered again, "What the hell man?" He looked real sickly and weakened. He had been sweating profusely, through his uniform. Honestly, he looked a little too sick to even be in uniform. His eyes were dark and had a real sunken in look, like he hadn't slept for days.

Higgins asked me, "You ok? You look a little lost today... everything alright, brotha!" He hacked a gnarly cough into his hand.

I looked at him with a puzzled, probably slightly disgusted look, and pulled my face back.

"Yeah. I'm fine, man. Just feeling a little lost with all that's going on lately, that's all. Are you ok man? You don't look so hot, either."

"Yeah, I'm fine. Ain't nothing," Higgins hacked out his response into hand. "I just got a little cold that's all. I'm fine! I'll power through it like I always do." Despite his reassurances, I knew something was wrong. As he put his hand on the window of the car, the moisture on his hand left a print on the window. He coughed again and tried to get out his farewell.

"Have a good day dude. You go ahead and come back to earth, huh!" Officer Higgins said, giggling a little at his own joke, holding his ribs gingerly. I looked at his sweaty handprint on the window with disgust, questioning if whatever he had was contagious.

"Yeah, yeah, yeah for sure!" I said with a fake giggle. As he let go of the window, the outline of his sweaty hand lingered. I instantly felt like I was sick, nodding my head as I pulled out of the parking lot. Officer Higgins waved at me and doubled over with his coughs as he walked away. Before pulling off completely I reached for the antibacterial wipes I had in my glove department. I wiped the window and then grabbed another, one wiping my hands till they were sore. My radio beeped off "6161, 10-54 possible dead body reported by multiple witnesses, 6161 proceed with caution." I picked up my mic to respond to the call. I sat there, stuck in my mind, pausing for a second and finally replied, "10-4. Officer Maestas on route. Please send me the location" The thought of Higgins' sickness lingered in the back of my mind. Gross. "10-23, Stand by 6161", dispatch replied back. I flicked my sirens on and sped down the road preparing for what would happen next. The way things had been going, there was no telling what was ahead of me

CASTLE CAGE

7

I turned the wheel hard around the corner, putting on my game face, as I began pulling into the parking lot. The darkness around me made everything about that call just that much more creepy and put me at unease. I pulled up to the building slowly, finally pulling the car to a stop. I let it idle for a moment, instinctually hesitant to get out of the vehicle. I knew something was going to be fucked up about this call. I could feel it deep down in my gut. I reached over, grabbing the shifter tightly and shoved my squad car into park. I took a deep breath, trying to figure out why I was feeling like such a rookie. The blue and red lights of my squad car lit up the parking lot of the apartment complex. All of the neighborhood stood around, huddling around the car. I shook my head, taking another deep breath, as I got out of the car and reached for my mic; placing my right hand on my gun, popping the holster open.

"10-97, just arrived at the scene, 10-23 stand by."

Dispatch responded, "10-4, standing by."

As I walked to the front of the apartment building, one woman ran up to me in a panic, "She's in there. I just opened the door to check on her and she was laying there covered in blood. I didn't know what to do," she frantically yelled in my face.

"Ma'am, calm down. Please step back and let me do my job. Everything is going to be fine, just please step back!" I firmly answered back, pushing her out of my way, while opening the narrow door to the front of the building. The mix of different smells wafted in my face. I drew my gun, holding it firmly in my hands. I think I was squeezing it so tightly the blood left my fingers. I could feel that something wasn't right. I couldn't take any chances after what the hell happened McAllister and based on the one news report I had seen. I cautiously walked down the dark narrow hallway, further and further as I continued walking down the cold, dark, dingy hallway. I was forced to breathe the pungent smell of cat piss and stale cigarettes. I could have sworn that I smelled a hint of spoiled milk. The smells were so strong it was hard not to gag. The further down the hallway I went, the thicker the smell got. The lights barely enough to light the hallway. The lights from my squad car flashed through the glass window of the front door. The light bulb hanging from the ceiling flickering on and off. It was eerie as fuck. Oddly, there wasn't a soul in sight. The sound of a TV blasted from down the hallway, echoing through the thin walls. I paced myself as I walked down the hallway, coming to a spiral staircase. I cringed as I noticed the ten flights of stairs.

"Fuck me. Of course she would be at the damn top." I muttered more expletives under my breath, shaking my head in disappointment. I reached for the flashlight on my belt. That damn thing was heavier than my gun. The flashlight flickered on and off and I smacked it against the wall as I raised it next to my gun. My heart pounded through my chest as I began to carefully take one step at a time. I slid along the God forsaken walls that barely held up the place.

Suddenly, I heard a loud, unexplained banging sound echoing from down the hallway. It sounded like it was coming from the fourth or fifth floor. With my guard up, I sprinted up the stairs to reach the fourth floor, skipping every other step, slamming my shoulder into the wall.

"Denver PD!" I shouted in a firm voice from down the hallway, trying to catch my breath. In all my years of being a police officer, I'd never been this nervous, my sweaty hands lost grip on my gun. I wiped them on my pant legs. The rustling from down the hallway continued. I shouted once again, "Denver PD! Come out with your hands up!" Still no response, but the banging continued. "Denver PD!" I shouted firmly. "Step out with your hands up! Now!" A door at the end of the hallway slammed open, swinging against the wall, violently bouncing off the wall before slamming closed again. Yelling out down the hallway I barked orders, "I'm only going to say this one more time. Denver Police Department! Step out of the apartment with both hands up! Now!" I shuffled closer to the front door of the apartment, the rustling continued. Suddenly, a shriek like I have never heard before sounded from behind the apartment door, startling the fuck out of me. My eyes wouldn't stop blinking. The sweat from my brow dripped into my eye. I stepped back against the wall. I tried to mentally prepare myself as a faint hiss came from behind the door. The light from the apartment was dim. The hissing from behind the door got more aggressive. I tried to convince myself that it was just a dog and all the shit was in my mind. I gave it one more chance and shakily shouted, "Denver Police Department! Step out from behind the door and put your hands up!" I gave up my stance, took a deep breath, quickly paced back and forth, and reset my position. I was scared to shit knowing full well that I was about to face the same shit as I had with McAllister. A loud shriek came from behind the door; the sound of furniture moved around in the apartment, along with heavy footsteps running away from the door.

I reached for the knob, but my hand slipped off, covered in a black bio, that smelled horrible. I quickly turned the doorknob, swinging the door open and never lowering my weapon. The lamp that had caused the crashing sound rolled around, rocking back and forth. The apartment was pitch black, the light bulb from the lamp shattered all over the floor. Again, the sweat from my brow was so heavy that my eyes started to burn. My heart pounded so hard that I thought I was going to have a heart attack right on the spot. A loud screaming shriek echoed from the dark hallway, followed by a loud thump that shook the whole apartment. I fell backwards in my shock, tripping on shredded carpet at the edge of the door, stumbling back towards the wall.

"Denver PD! Put your hands up, step out of the room and place your hands on your head." More thumping sounded from across the apartment hallway: thump, thump, thump. After building up the balls, I rushed fully into the apartment hallway. My nerves were so intense that I began to hyperventilate. Anxiety prevented me from catching my breath and again: thump, thump, thump. Something moved heavily from across the apartment.

"Damin it! Denver PD! PUT YOUR HANDS UP, STEP OUT WHERE I CAN SEE YOU, PUT YOUR HANDS ON YOUR HEAD. I'M NOT GOING TO SAY IT AGAIN. I WILL SHOOT!"

Cautiously, I walked down the hallway, in the dark apartment. My right foot hit something slick and slid into the wall. I used the wall to brace myself, flashing the light down at my foot, where a puddle of blood soaked into the wooden floors. The pictures from the wall were smashed on the ground, bloody handprints smeared all the way down the hallway, along with footprints. The banging got louder as I crept through the hallway. I came to a pause, the sweat just seemed to pour out of me. It was dead quiet; too quiet. The bedroom door viciously swung open, slamming into the wall. Behind it, a crazed, elderly woman stood in the doorway, staring me down. As she hissed and growled, like an animal, her teeth chattered rapidly, black bio and saliva drizzled down her chin. Her short, thin, white hair covered half of her face, black bio dripped from her mouth onto the top of her feet. She didn't stay still for long. She was anything but frail as she ran out of the room, sprinting from 0 to 60, slamming her whole body into the wall; her feet slid across the puddles of blood in the hallway. The elderly lady stopped for a minute, her eyes glaring deeply at me, her teeth chattered, as she put herself in what seemed to be an attack mode.

She seemed focused on my presence, her head snapping; the bones in her neck popping and crackling as she twisted her neck into what seemed to be agonizing positions. It was like her neck was disconnected from her body. She snapped her teeth together, the muscles in her face pulled. She bit down on her teeth with so much anger as she stared me down. She stood at the end of the hallway in a charge stance, her long fingers snapped with each muscle spasm in her hands. Her teeth clenched so tightly that her teeth began to break. I was sure that if she was the same as the other two victims I would have to shoot her ass. The sounds she made were the same as what I'd heard from the old man and his granddaughter. She had the same symptoms: blood and saliva dripping from her mouth and body twitching uncontrollably. Her teeth showed like a dog being cornered; growling and hissing, her head whipping back and to the side. The sound of her neck popping and crackling instantly sent chills down my spine. All she had on was her night gown and it was covered in blood. Her shoulder dislocated itself from the socket, popping and crackling.

"Ma'am, stay back. Are you injured? Do I need to call an ambulance?"

I really had hoped that she was sane enough to answer my question, but I knew at the back of my mind that she was just another crazy bitch that I did not want to shoot, but would have to. Her head twitched and jerked.

"Ma'am are you ok? Denver PD," I tried to give her every chance I could. I didn't want to have to shoot her, but in the same regard maybe she was giving me the chance to shoot her ass without a fight. She got restless, stomped like a bull. She was ready to charge. She sprinted down the hallway, screaming at the top of her lungs, swinging her arms at me with enormous ferocity and speed. Pop, pop! I fired two shots into her chest, neither of which had any effect on her. She leapt at me, tackling me from the hallway into her kitchen, tripping me into the refrigerator. The old woman grabbed my head with both hands barring her fingers on the top of my skull, wrapping her fingers through my hair, bludgeoning my head against the fridge. The flash bang of my head slamming against the fridge caused my finger to pull the trigger shooting off a random shot. Pieces of ceiling debris fell on top of us as we struggled. I tried to get another round into her. My gun went off. Pop! I had missed, shooting the ceiling, as we both fell onto her kitchen table, knocking off a plate of food and condiments. I struggled with her on top of me. She was so powerful, trying to claw at me, attempting to dig her fingers into my eyes. Blood was smeared all over my face as I held her off. That woman had to have been in her seventies or eighties, but she fought with the strength of trained, male, fighter in his twenties.

I dropped my gun to the floor to gain leverage. Her teeth chomped at anything close to her mouth. I used my body weight to barrel roll us both off of the table and land on top of her. Again, the blow didn't even phase her. Nothing stopped her clawing and scratching. The blood on her hands slipped off my uniform. She hissed and kicked at me. I held her down with my hands planted on her neck and chest. Her head snapped at me, desperate to bite my arm as I arm-barred her neck and attempted to reach for my gun with the other hand. I lost my leverage after reaching for my gun. After I lost my grip on her neck, without hesitation, I started punching her in the face as hard as I could. Her head slammed back on the floor, cracking the back of her head on the ground. My fist tightened and I swung my fist at her with all that I had, punching her in the eyes and the mouth. Her front teeth broke with each punch. The elderly woman's head snapped back into the floor again, cracking the tile, before finally lying there limp.

I took a deep breath, staring at her warily. She'd made no movement, not even a breath. I couldn't believe that I'd had to beat the shit out of a little old woman. As I stood, I spit out the blood that accumulated in my own mouth from being hit so forcefully. I bent over, grabbed my flashlight and aimed it toward the little old woman; in complete disbelief at what had happened. I worried about how I would explain this to anyone. I had killed two unarmed, frail elderly civilians and a young girl in a matter of two days. I grabbed my radio to report everything to home base, but had no clue what I'd say. Shit, I'd been manhandled by a seventy year old woman in a nightgown.

"6161, 10-55, I don't know what the hell just happened, officer requesting assistance. 11-44, requesting medical assistance, non-urgent" No answer. Radio static squeaked and popped through the mic.

I repeated myself, "6161,10-55, officer in need of assistance and 11-44, also requesting medical assistance." I walked toward the door, exhausted and confused. The dim light from the hallway continued to dim off and on. Just as I was about to walk out the door, I heard: thump, thump, thump. I turned around as fast as I could, shining my flashlight into the apartment. I took a deep, frustrated breath and reluctantly walked back into the apartment, shining my light in the kitchen where the old woman had been. She was gone. The puddle of blood on the kitchen floor had slide marks to another opening in the hallway. I drew my gun once again and swung my light scanning everywhere. Again, more thump, thump, thumping footsteps. She had been running around the house as if she was playing a game with me. I could hear her faint breathing, as she hissed and growled softly. I moved cautiously (fuck I had been so drained in that moment) into the front room. More footsteps, no sign of her. My heart couldn't take anymore. I was sure that I was going to have a damn heart attack. My body felt like it had been shot up with endless amounts of adrenaline. As I made a pass with my light through the living room, rapid footsteps came hauling ass behind me. Fuck.

The elderly woman leapt off the coffee table before I could get a shot off. Without hesitation, she flew through the air, throwing my body to the ground like a scared little kid. She picked me up, flopping me around like a rag doll and smashed me into the ground. As she flew toward me again, I kicked up my feet and launched her through the window at the end of the hallway. Screaming violently, she plummeted out of the 10th floor window. I could hear her land on top of a car. The sound of glass shattering and crunching metal was eerily noisy amid the silence outside. I took a deep breath before getting up to look out the window. Of course. She had landed on my damn squad car, crushing the top of it, shattering my lights. I'd never been so pissed, but figured that might mean I'd get the new Dodge Charger I'd been requesting.

I shook my head in disappointment and muttered, "This night just gets better and better." I grabbed my mic and continued to attempt to reach headquarters. I still received only static in response.

8

My head spun as I looked at my watch and made my way downstairs. It was 11:45pm. Marcy should have been there. I couldn't figure out what the hell was going on. I was deep in thought as I walked out of the building. My car was completely crushed. I couldn't have driven it. Considering that the steering wheel was snapped from the steering column, driving may have proven to be difficult. The streets were dead, nobody was in sight. Not a single car drove by. I wondered to myself, 'What the fuck? Did I miss something?' No matter which direction that I looked, there was nothing. The only movement around me was the changing of the traffic light from green to yellow to red. Not a sound; no dogs, music, engines, *nothing* . There had been nosy ass people standing out there not twenty minutes before. I shook my head in confusion; still trying to reach headquarters. Nothing but static.

I realized I'd have to make the trek back to the station by foot. I grabbed my shotgun from out of the car, the old lady still lying there on top of my hood, her hand still twitching. I threw the shotgun onto my back and popped the clip to see how many rounds I had left in my 9mm. I jogged to the police station. It was really eerie to not see anybody around. As I paused to catch my breath and assess the situation around me, the sound of an engine roared from down the street, shooting through the red light at about 80 miles per hour. It was gone just as fast as it had appeared. I resumed running. Fuck, I was so out of shape from all the drinking. I couldn't breath after the first block. I *had* to get to the station.

CHAPTER 6

The Police Station

Off in the distance I could hear gunfire and people shouting. At least I could hear something! The police station was only a few more blocks. I turned the corner onto Perry Street, pacing myself, so my debilitated ass didn't keel over. A crowd of people showed up out of nowhere, running past me to meet up with another crowd that stood in the streets. In a matter of about 10 seconds, the streets were filled with people evacuating and rioting. Houses and businesses were literally burning everywhere that I looked.

"What the fuck?" I spoke aloud. A large number of people were shooting at one another, fighting over the things they were stealing from nearby stores. People were getting trampled. I couldn't see any of my fellow officers on scene. I was unclear if there were more crazed people like the old woman, or not. Hell had appeared to have broken out in a forty five minute span and I was suddenly right in the middle of it. There was no way to run from it. Everything evil in the world came to light and there was nothing anyone could do about it. I felt like I needed to do something, but what was I supposed to do? Take on every person in The Denver Metro Area with a gun, or every infected person, on my own? I could barely handle that old woman alone. It would have been impossible. My adrenaline was still heavily pumping through my entire body, my mind on alert. An Arab couple pushed their way through the crowd, shouting words I did not understand, waving their arms at me. The Arab woman reached over at me, pulling at my arm, screaming hysterically. She was speaking Arabic. I pulled my arm away, gently putting my hands up to calm her down. The woman tried broken English. She kept repeating something about her baby; over and over, frantically. The more frantic that she became, the less I understood her.

The husband pointed his finger in my chest, shouting above all the noise, he too, attempted broken English to communicate. Both of them tugged at me, but with everything that had happened, I was hesitant.

"I'm sorry. I don't know what you're saying. Please, slow down, ma'am." I stood there, trying to understand what she was saying, trying to calm her down. In the distance I heard screeching tires coming in our direction. I swiveled my head around quickly, to see a red Honda that was just inches away obliterating us. It crushed through the crowd of people, flinging bodies like dandelion seeds. The chaos around us erupted like a volcano. Gunshots popped off from multiple directions. From the crowd of people, attempted to protect themselves. It was hard to absorb everything that was going on. The law didn't matter anymore. I was the law and it meant nothing. There was no way for me to help. It was everyone for themselves. The red Honda lost control down the street, bouncing off another parked car, the sound of crunching metal rang out over the hysteria of the crowd. The car flipped on its side, rolling over all of the innocent people in its path a clear sense of mob mentality was in effect. The gaping hole in the crowd revealed how many infected fill the streets. A swarm of them chased after the rolling car. The woman driving the car was immediately ejected out of the driver window, her limp body still in the street. The car continued without her, landing against several gas pumps and igniting. In a powerful display of Hollywood style drama, the gas station burst into flames. I was actually pretty surprised by how quickly it all happened.

The blaze burned so hotly that it felt like it was singeing my facial hair off from across the street. The flames leveled everything in their path, igniting anything and anyone, standing close. The entire left end of the block was consumed. I felt the heat on my face intensify with each roaring explosion. One of the explosions was close enough to force me to the ground, knocking the wind out of me. The Arabic couple next to me were thrown a couple of feet away. The husband picked up his wife and they panicked, running in the opposite direction of the chaos. I laid there for a couple of seconds, while pieces of debris soared through the air. The lucky people who had survived came to their feet and scrambled around in a greater panic than before. The infected seemed unphased by the blaze and were taking people out left and right, as they ran in panic. Agonizing screams thickened the air. The smell of burning flesh and gasoline was horrible. My ears rang from the blast, then a gunshot went off right next to my ear, enhancing my deafness. I was shaken to the core. The ringing reverberated through my skull making it hard for me to concentrate. My chest felt caved in as I tried to catch my breath. My legs felt like jello as I attempted to climb to my feet, breathing deeply. The pressure of the explosion was so intense it had felt as if I'd been smashed by a truck.

A woman walked up to me, her back on fire. She looked deep into my eyes. She had the look of the infected, the crazed, her eyes were blood infused and she hissed and chomped her teeth.

The foam in her mouth was plastered in the edges of her mouth. Her hair was incinerated, leaving raw, burned flesh on the top of her head and face. I gagged a bit at the smell. The infected woman, completely unaware she was on fire, charged at me. I could see the skin on her face popping and bubbling to a black crisp, rolling back from the bone, cooking slowly. She growled viciously lunging at me and violently waving her arms. I reached for my pistol, only to find that it was missing from its holster. I frantically looked around on the ground for any sign of it. I found it a couple of inches away. I reached for it and fired off a couple rounds into her neck. The bullets entered through her jugular and exited out of the back of her neck, along with a pink mist that was quickly incinerated by the fire. Blood squirted out of the front of her neck like a river. I breathed deeply and slowly squeezed the trigger once again, shooting her directly in the eye. The side of her head exploded. The chunks of her skull that exploded off flopped to the ground, still sizzling from the fire. Her knees buckled from under her; once flailing arms limply fell to her side. She fell heavily to the ground.

The sound of the gun shots got the attention of more of the infected. Two of them quickly climbed to their feet running at me. One screamed as he sprinted, lunging at me as I shot him in the head directly; bringing him down immediately. He'd been charging with such speed and force that he continued to roll across the pavement, even after being shot. Multiple infected chased after him as he rolled away. The infected seemed to fall in line with each other as they caught sight of me. More and more joined the sprint to attack me. I fired as accurately and quickly as I could, dropping several before they jumped on top of me.

Their lifeless bodies were piling up next to me and more were coming. I was in a prone position. I knew that I had to move, but I was so exhausted and they came so quickly. I tried to roll away. My eyes locked with the eyes of one of the dead; they were lifeless, but wide open. I fired some more shots as I rolled, but the click of my gun was a gut wrenching sound in that moment. Empty. I jumped to my feet and came face to face with an infected man. I used the butt of my gun to crush his skull repeatedly. He fell against me, sliding to the ground and leaving a streak of blood along my uniform.

I was actually really surprised that it was that easy taking them down one by one. They were coming so fast, though. I needed supplies. I wouldn't have enough to last long without my squad car. I almost felt like a badass as one came from behind and gripped my shoulder. I instinctively flipped the small little Asian lady over me. I could feel her tiny teeth ripping from the back of my bullet proof vest. I slammed her easily to the ground and stomped my foot on her shoulder, planting her into the ground and squeezing off a shot in the middle of her forehead. I dropped that bitch like a fat kid dropped his ice cream on a hot day. All that adrenaline running through my body was insane. I even had a splash of confidence as I walked away. It wasn't long lasting, however, as I attempted to move and my knee twisted in pain and buckled beneath me. Of course.

2

I had to drag my right leg, making it impossible to run. It was immensely swollen. I pulled another clip from my belt and loaded it before any more of those psycho infected fucks showed up. The closer I got to the police station, the more I realized that I didn't know what to expect. If the radio communication was down, what had happened to everyone there? Questions started rolling in my head. I had no idea if I was about to walk into an ambush, or if everyone was okay and just fighting the good fight. I also weighed the chance that my colleagues might be shooting everything that approached the station and they might just take my ass out.

Shortly after I removed myself from the crowd of chaos over on Perry Street, I came across empty silence again. Just two streets over not a soul was in sight. The streets were dead quiet. Home's windows were blacked out. I still kept my head on a swivel as I walked up to a park. It was eerily quiet and I wasn't sure if I should just keep to the street or take a shortcut through the park.

3

With my leg being the way it was, I knew that I needed to take the shortcut. I was so close to the station, but going around the park would take too long. Nevertheless, it was so dark and not the smartest way. My knee was weak and shaky, each step left me with a burning sensation rolling up my leg. I limped through the park, ready and waiting for a fight to begin. I approached the bridge that led across the lake. I looked around, knowing it would be a bad idea to cross it. What if those things trapped me in the middle and I had nowhere to go?

But I had no choice with my leg being so weak. I cautiously approached the bridge. As I walked, I heard a faint splash and poised for a fight. I looked down over the bridge railing and with the moonlight shining overhead, I got a sense of peace amid the chaos. I saw fish swimming about like nothing had happened; nothing affected their world. My peace was shattered suddenly, though, as they scattered like something scared them off. Shortly after they scattered, a line of bubbles arose in their place. The faint image of a face protruded from the darkness of the bottom of the lake and the body of a woman slowly floated up, almost leveling with the line of water. Her eyes were closed, her golden hair swirled with each rippling wave that passed over her face. Her body floated there, still in the water, the moonlight reflecting off her pale white skin. I leaned further over the railing to get a better look, but she slowly drifted back down to the darkness. It was honestly the most unnerving thing that I had ever seen. I had to move. I couldn't waste any more time.

4

My heart was heavy for the young lady in the lake. A sense of sympathy grew deeper in my chest and opened up a door that had been locked for a long time. All those feelings and emotions washed over me as they had on the day I'd lost Jenny and Carson. That girl in the lake couldn't have been more than 16 years old, maybe even younger.

No one was there to protect her, no one had kept her safe, or she would have been alive. As I walked more questions started digging their way into my head. Where had her parents been? No one had been there for her and I hadn't been there for Jenny and Carson. I hadn't been there to protect them. No one was there to save them. I hadn't been there and I hadn't been there to save the little girl in the lake. I don't know why, but there was some type of relation and I felt crushed by the weight of my guilt. I dropped to my knees and sobbed. My heart and mind searched for closure. I knew that they were gone, but I'd had no closure. I'd been deadened to the thought that they were never coming back.

For whatever reason, I'd found my closure in that horrendous moment atop the bridge in the middle of the apocalypse. I had made my peace with it. I knew that I would never get over them, but my heart had finally accepted the finality of it all. Whether the world came to its end, or I made it through somehow, I knew I was going to be ok. I let the moment wash over, concerned with nothing else. Then I climbed to my feet sniffling and crying like a baby. I can't explain why, but I began firing shots into a nearby tree, splintering its bark in a shower of emotion. As I got closer, I leaned on the tree for support.

I'd never cried that hard. My face washed with tears; snot blobbed out of my nose. I took a deep, introspective breath. It was time to move on.

CASTLE CAGE

5

As I emerged from the park into the east side of Denver's streets I ran into crowds of people attempting to leave the city. Most had no choice but to abandon their cars. There was too much traffic to move. The highways were packed with abandoned vehicles. The virus was spreading so fast that hardly anyone could get out. The military hadn't had any time to react. More and more sane people crowded themselves around me, asking for help. I didn't know what to do, or say.

"Things will be fine, go back to your homes and lock the doors. Help will come soon." I didn't think that help would actually come. But, I said that to everyone who asked me for help. All these men and women looked at me for comfort, to be their savior, their eyes hopeful. Dying with hope seemed better than the alternative, so I lied over and over again.

I could finally see the station through the crowd. As I neared the doors, the behavior of the crowd changed. They were bashing out windows; looting and rioting, attacking one another. Greedy people were ripping children from cars in their attempt to escape. On the corner, a little girl stood screaming for her mommy, holding her bear in her hand, still in her pajamas. A woman ran across to the little girl, attempting to calm her down, then forcefully picking her up, cuddling her in her arms. She ran down an alleyway, followed by a hoard of infected. I had to do something! I shoved people out of my way. When I got to the alley, it was too late. A group of infected had already nearly devoured the little girl and had their way with her mother. I couldn't bear to watch, so I turned away.

The streets were mixed with infected and civilians. A tall, skinny figure in a hoodie, with a bandana covering his face, dressed in black from head to toe, ran through the crowd swinging a baseball bat at anything that was in his path. The whites of his eyes showed through the blackness of his face, his arms cocked back, gripping the base of the baseball bat as he swung at me. I ducked my head and the baseball bat hit the parked car next to me; busting the driver side window.

"Fuck the police! Fuck you pig!" I lunged my hand into his throat, swiping his leg from under him and slammed his ass to the ground. The air from his lungs quickly evacuated. I placed my knee into his chest, drew out my gun and stuck it to his head. I expected him to be a grown man, but he was just a kid. A kid who wasn't close to passing for 17. Immediately fear took over that kid and the bottom of my pant leg filled with warmth. The little fucker pissed on me. My pants leg soaked it up like a sponge. I was so fucking pissed. It took everything in my body to not pull the trigger.

Maybe it was mob mentality setting in, but I squeezed his throat with my hand. I could feel his vertebrae on my finger tips. The young man tried to get words out as I squeezed tighter.

"Fuck you man!" he stubbornly choked out. An Explosion roared behind me, causing me to flinch and lose my grip on his neck. I turned my head back to see what the hell had happened. A car had exploded. Suddenly, the kid's right fist swung over, punching me in the side of my temple, dazing the shit out of me. I let him go and fell over, my head spinning. He took over after spitting at me and although I was tempted to shoot his stupid ass, I was seeing three of him and couldn't even if I'd desperately wanted to. My confidence was shaken. I got put on my ass by a kid and I'd done nothing about it.

Infected were having a free for all. They began charging at me from every which way. It wasn't long before each one that had its attention on me changed their focus to the poor son of a bitch standing in their way. It was a massacre. Anyone who tried to escape was a sitting duck, in the middle of a war zone. From men to women, right down to children, the bloodbath of the century ensued. They devoured anything they could and I was in the damn middle of it. Out of the crowd, bulldozing everyone, came a giant of an infected man. He focused on me like I was a Wendy's sign, flashing in the middle of darkness, and his fat ass was hungry. He was hungry for a pig and I was that pig; his eyes were infused with blood. He fixated on me and I prepared myself to be his bitch. The rest of the infected backed off like they knew their place. It was like a pack of lions, ready to gorge, but backing off for the alpha to eat first. Bite marks covered his entire body, chunks of flesh were missing from each side of his gigantic arms. His muscle shirt was soaked with his blood and that of his victims. His mouth gushed black bio and his eyes were so infused with blood that he appeared to cry bloody tears. His teeth chattered violently as he rushed through the crowd of infected, pinning me against the car, my back digging into the broken glass. He forced himself on me violently. That fucker was strong. My arms felt like noodles. He pressed his head towards me, mouth wide open, his breath smelled like decayed flesh. Blood dripped from his mouth, mixed with rotted stomach bio; the smell was all too familiar. I resisted with all the might that I had left, but his teeth sank into my vest, biting right through the fabric and into the kevlar. I screamed out loud, sure that I was going to get bitten. That was it for me. I couldn't push him back and he was ripping through my vest like it was tissue paper. His hands were strong and in no way was I able to break from his grip. One of his brute fists swung, punching me right in the forehead. My head quickly bounced off of the car to meet his hammer of a hand again. The flash of white blinded me momentarily. The world began to spin. I sloppily shoved the barrel of my gun into his forehead smashing it over and over till the skin on his head split wide open. I couldn't see, only feel, his head and I hit with all the rage that I'd had trapped inside of me. Nothing. It did absolutely nothing. His head snapped backwards, preparing to come into my jugular. His breath was so pungent that it made me want to vomit in the middle of our battle. My back bent inward against the car. The infected brute smashed me into the door of the car.

 I wedged the barrel of the gun into the small of his throat where the jaw meets the chin and squeezed the trigger; the hammer clicked, empty. The fucking thing was empty. I used the gun in his neck and the car behind me as leverage to push him back. With his resistance and mine, the gun dug deeper into his throat and blood began flowing over my hand. The infected brute clenched his jaw, trying to push against the gun barrel. I could feel whatever was in his neck snapping; tendons and cartilage separated. I had gained enough distance from him to wedge my knee in between our bodies. I used the car as leverage again, shoving him away from me. The gun pulled out of his neck as he stumbled back. I reached for the clips on my belt, but the brute came to his feet quickly. I had one clip left. The infected man lunged at me just as I replaced the clip. I pulled my arm back, using the side of his head to cock the gun. I accidentally ripped his ear off as the gun slid downward. He ripped pieces of my vest and shirt away from me. Flipping the gun so that my thumb was on the trigger, I planted the barrel to the top of his big ass bald head and fired. The gun bounced up as it fired and twisted my wrist in agony. The bullet blasted through his skull and out his chin, right into my vest.

The air evacuated from my lungs with the shot. His dead body flopped to the ground. The bullet had almost pierced point blank into my chest as shredded as it was. If it hadn't been for his big ass head, I think it would have just gone all the way through. The goop of his brains stained the front of my chest. It hurt so fucking badly to take the bullet at such close range. I couldn't breathe at all and I dropped to the ground, rolling in agony. I had to get to the station. God, I was so out of shape.

6

Fighting that big son of a bitch took everything that I'd had left. His teeth still hung on the cloth of my vest. Exhausted and weak, I wasn't sure if i was going to make it across the street to the police station. I stumbled my way through the crowd of people trying to escape the city. Above me, news choppers watched the dead eat the flesh of the living. The virus had spread so vastly that the infected outnumbered the living.

As far as the eyes could see the feeding frenzy was rampant. Humanity was gone and it was survival of the fittest mode. The stampede of infected trampled over the living, taking them out quickly. Two children screamed for help and for their parents; pounding their fists against the windows. Three infected jumped on the back window of the car, breaking out the back window; pulling out the two little children and savagely ripped to shreds. Silence. From around the corner, thousands of the infected ran at the remaining living. A clash between infected and living; a bloody war zone of gnashing and clawing erupted. Everyone died. Monster or human, they dropped like flies. I ran as fast as I could, weaving in and out of the commotion. I tripped over the sidewalk and splatted onto the concrete.

With no remorse, or empathy, for me the living ran over me trying to escape their doom. Feet planted into my back, feeling like a million daggers stabbing me. I fell into blackness.

I came to, in a panic and tried to leap up. I felt heavy. I couldn't seem to move. The knot on the back of my head throbbed at the base of my skull. I pushed myself up, gasping for air, waiting for something to attack me. I realized that I was covered with dead bodies. I was surrounded by dead bodies and limbs that had been torn away. As I rose from the ground, a random torso slid off of me. A head rolled on the sidewalk, the jaw twitched open, then shut.

Her eyes rolled to the back of her skull while blood flowed from her eye sockets.

I'd seen plenty of crime scenes to know when a head was pulled or cut from the spine. It was all too familiar, but all too different at the same time. I screamed, lost in time, but quickly covered my mouth in fear that one of those things would be able to hear me, or maybe the damn flood of those bastards would come back. I muffled my own candy ass screams. In a panic, I backed myself up against a store front. The scene was indescribable: limbs and body parts made mountains on the street. Everything in sight was covered in blood and bio. The top of the car next to me showed the half eaten body of a dismembered man's torso.

7

Finally breaking away from the chaos, I reached the parking lot of the station. I made my way to the gate that surrounded the impound lot. I hoped that I would go unnoticed by crawling behind the bushes carefully toward the front gate. The guard station was in flames The front access gate was closed. A couple of infected stood in front of the gate to the parking lot. I hid behind the bushes. I sat there and watched their movements, briefly studying them through the bushes. They just stood there, completely unaware of my presence. One of the infected stared up to the sky with tears of blood running down her pale, sunken face.The other two stood beside one another, rocking back and forth, staring down at the ground, totally unaware of the world around them. The muscles in their faces twitched and nodded similarly to someone with Tourettes, but at the same time they were in shutdown mode. Their eyes were wide open, scanning back and forth, as you do when you dream vividly, and with black bio dripping from their mouths like teething babies. Except, they were not drooling babies. They were flesh eating machines, infected to kill anything and everything in sight. I sat there watching; observing them in silent awe.

My foot slid over, causing a rock to roll down onto the pavement. The clicking sound caught the attention of the infected, snapping them out of their daze. Their head snapped towards the sound of the rock. They sprinted over to the sound of the rock without any hesitation. With a quick, quiet reaction, I curled in a ball under the bushes. I quietly pulled my weapon, ready to fire. The group of the infected sprinted off past me into the street. They had quick reactions, but weren't so smart it seemed. I took my chance, jumping up from the bushes. It was all clear.

I ran to the gate only to find that it was jammed shut. Fuck! I jumped up to reach the bar on the top of the gate to see if I could pull myself over the gate. I gripped and pulled, but I was too weak.

God, I was so fucking out of shape. I laughed for a moment, picturing myself doing one armed pull-ups with a glass of scotch in my other hand. I searched for another possible way in. And, it was easier than I'd thought. A part of the fence was torn down. Skid marks led up to the gaping hole in the fence. A police car was flipped on its top, burning. The police cruiser had wrecked into the parked vehicles of the lot. I walked through the hole. The scene was more gruesome than I'd even imagined. From the look of it, the police cruiser had wiped out every police officer in its way, scraping their bodies across the pavement in the parking lot. A cadet's body was pinned between the wrecked car and one of the parked cruisers. His head was smashed to pieces like a melon from the impact. My focus was completely on the burning cruiser as I made my way through the scene. My foot kicked something heavy, the sound of it making a squishing, thudding sound. When I looked down I saw that it was the arm of another cadet. The stitched badge on the sleeve of the mangled arm read: DENVER COUNTY POLICE DEPARTMENT CADET PROGRAM. I had to close my eyes from the horror. My memory bank was fully stocked with traumatic images at that point. The cruiser's number was 2189. That was Officer Miller's cruiser. That most likely meant that my friend was gone. Blood was wiped all over the side panels of the car. Chunks of the smashed head of the cadet spackled the bumper.

Off in the distance I heard shrieking. It startled me. I placed both hands on my 9mm ready to shoot anything that came at me. Puddles of blood flooded the parking lot. Inch by inch was covered in blood. It was painted all over the parking lot. The stairs were like a waterfall of blood. My firearm was charged and ready. I bent and grabbed a few extra clips that were scattered from the downed officers. I cautiously walked to the door; the front window was shattered to pieces, bloody handprints covered the frame of the door. I couldn't help but wonder where all the other police officers were. Surely someone had survived. Fuck, we'd been trained for emergencies. How was it possible that none of those pussies could make it through the chaos? Not one was in sight, though.

I stepped over the broken glass into the front lobby. The sound of the chaos going on outside was really hard to ignore. I was terrified, waiting for one of those fuckers to jump at me at any second. I could hear a faint growling quietly reverberating. It sounded like it was all around me. I kept looking around; my head swiveled, but I still could not find where it was coming from. I came around Officer Lopez' desk. A puddle of blood slowly spread outward from under the desk. The top of the desk was covered in blood. I noticed some movement coming from the stack of papers that had fallen over. Whatever it was, it was pulsating, moving the stack of papers on the desk.

I was honestly scared to shit to look under the desk. I timidly moved closer to the desk and with the tip of my shoe, cautiously moved the stack of papers. As the papers moved, a strand of brown hair appeared. Then, a chunk of flesh, which was attached to the hair. I bent over to take a closer look. It was a chunk of flesh from a woman's scalp. The hairy chunk of flesh pulsated, the muscles in the chunk of scalp twitched, moving just like a heartbeat. With the barrel of my gun, I poked at the chunk of flesh. Black goop oozed out like I'd popped a zit. The smell of it activated my gag reflex and I puked up the yellow goop from the bottom of my stomach. I wretched violently. My throat tightened; the veins in my neck felt like they were going to burst. I kicked away the chunk of flesh, sliding across the floor.

The power buzzed and shut off. Pitch black filled the entire office. A loud machine like sound buzzed from the basement as the backup generator started up. The LED's kicked in. Behind one of the officer's desks a stack of papers fell off the side, causing an echoing thud, followed by thumping footsteps. I wasn't waiting this time to see what, or who, it was. I fired off two shots, aiming at the cubicle. I waited, but realized that my shots had given away from location. A shrieking filled the darkness behind the cubicles. It echoed and I couldn't tell where it came from. The footsteps started slowly, but picked up speed. I moved slowly, but a cadet with a missing arm came running out of the cubicles so fast that it still caught me off guard. He had his head down and he blasted into my side at maximum speed, tossing me into the cheap walls of the cubicles. I was like a wrecking ball moving through a brick wall. He was gone. I couldn't see him. I couldn't fucking see him. I spun around like a psycho trying to figure out where he was. A hand reached out from behind me, slamming my head back into the broken cubicle walls multiple times, gripping the top of my hair. Saliva and black goop spattered across my face. The cadet hissed fiercely through his teeth. I clenched my right fist, swinging it into the face of the infected cadet. I blasted him so hard in his temple that he doubled over, dead. His ass pointed up in the air; blood from his face painted the ground. I had the anger of 1000 pissed off men. I began stomping his head with my foot. Each blowing stomp crushed his head in. Over and over, I planted my foot into his head. His skull cracked, but I didn't want to stop. His head busted open, it didn't matter. I kept stomping his head until there was nothing left but a blob of mush. Then I kicked over his lifeless body. I screamed at the cadet with anger, fear and confidence mixed together. Emotions sped through my body until I tried to regulate my breathing.

I plopped my ass onto one of the desks and scanned the room to find my gun. My gun stuck out from under the infected cadet's body.

"Fuck you, you piece of shit!" I said, kicking his lifeless body, as I retrieved my gun. His jaw flung up into the air as his body tipped over.

The body rolled over into one of the cubicle walls, breaking in from the hinge that barely held it up, causing a huge creaking crashing sound. I flinched and waited to see if there was any reaction. Yep. A screaming roar from another infected filled the hallway, coming in my direction. I ran over to Ronda's desk to check the cameras, but the power of out. The tip of my finger touched a half-eaten pink donut. It saddened me to see the pink donut. Not knowing whether your friends are dead or alive was a heavy feeling. I knew that Erik had brought Ronda that donut at the beginning of his shift. He brought her one every day. A thumping sound came from around the corner. A faint gurgle, followed by the sound of hissing got louder as it got closer. I pushed the chair away and squeezed my big body under that small ass desk. The hissing got closer. I held my breath, trying not to make any movement, hoping the infected would come and leave. The infected shuffled past Ronda's desk. With my gun cocked, I got ready to take out whoever it was. The foot of the infected walked next to the desk, blood droplets dripped from above. The feet shuffled clumsily, smearing the blood across the tile floor. A noise came from a distance, catching the attention of the infected, as it ran off to chase the new sound. I let some time pass by before peeking my head out to see if it was clear. I thought it was clear, but a loud shriek came from the top of the desk as I peeked my head out. The infected stood by the right side of the desk and reached over to grab at me. I rolled back under the desk and fired through the desk, hoping it would hit. I unloaded my clip from under the desk. The wood of the desk splintered with each shot before the infected fell dead on top of the desk. The infected's face was completely painted with bullets, mangled to the point of unrecognition.

'Damn. I'm a better shot than I thought,' I thought proudly. The back up lights flickered on and off. I needed to see if there were any survivors. I walked away from Ronda's desk with a confident strut, or maybe it was my busted ass knee...nah, I was cocky again. All I was missing was my black sunglasses. I passed by the Chief's office. The door was busted wide open, hanging off the hinges; the desk flipped on its side. I was shocked! That was a good 300 pound solid oak desk. Something crazy had to have happened. A faint gurgling sound coming from behind the desk.

"Chief...?" I asked as I walked slowly into the office. The gurgling growl got louder and louder as I got closer to the desk. I didn't notice the Chief's favorite bottle of scotch on the floor next to my foot and accidentally kicked it into the desk. I realized that I was the loudest mother fucker on the planet. The gurgling behind the desk instantly got quiet. I thought to myself, 'Fucking pay attention you idiot,'.

With my finger on the trigger, I called out again, "Chief?" I kept asking, but I knew it wasn't him.

"Chief?" The police station was dead quiet. The sweat precipitated through my vest and shirt. I wiped the sweat off of my face as I took a step closer to look behind the desk. As I came closer to the desk, I saw a scene that I wasn't expecting. An infected was chewing at the neck of the chief, pulling and tugging at the flesh. Ronda's head snapped up, a chunk of Chief Morrison hung from her mouth. She jumped up to her feet. She stepped out and started toward me, but she tripped on the scotch bottle and crashed face first into the filing cabinets.

I bolted. Officer Lopez chased after me. I ran into the lobby of the police station, so that I could get a clear shot. Ronda was just seconds behind me, grabbing my arm as I spun around. I grabbed the edge of her collar with my left hand, pushing her back and sticking the gun into the bottom of her jaw, pulling the trigger. The top of her head blew off. As I held Officer Lopez by her collar, I noticed the big chunk of flesh hanging from her neck. I tossed her lifeless body to the ground. I knew that wherever those things were, they'd heard the gunshots.

I looked around, trying to find any sign of survivors. I saw the light on in the hallway down to the basement. It dawned on me that there was a good chance that McAllister was alive. Nobody even went down there. so I knew it had to be him walking over to the stairs leading down stairs. I started down the stairs. Something flickered at the bottom of the stairs. I waved my flashlight back and forth, the reflection of something down at the bottom of the stairwell caught my attention. I took the stairs step by step, taking my time. I had my gun ready to fire. The shiny object looked like it might have been a badge. I knelt down, picked it up, wiping some of the blood away. It was Officer McAllister's. My heart sank a bit.

I tucked it into my pocket, shouting down the hallway, "McAllister!" I heard a faint call from the holding cells down the hallway. With relief, I started hauling ass down the hallway. Officer Stanley came rushing out of one of the holding rooms, his mouth covered in blood, his eyes bulging from his head. He ambushed me completely. Officer Stanley sprinted at me with lightning speed.

Pissed off at myself for letting my guard down, I spun and fired off shots! One of the shots hit him the shoulder, temporarily stunning him. I jumped back, but Officer Stanley recovered quickly. I squeezed the trigger one more time, sending another shot right into the top of his skull; the cap of his head flying off, snapping his neck in the process. Stanley fell to his knees, then flopped to the ground. The top of his head spilled on the tile floor. As I wiped my hands off, another call rang out of the holding cells. I passed Stanley's body lying on the floor; for a second, I thought I heard a gurgling sound coming from his body. His stomach looked bigger than usual. It looked like it was going to break open his buttons. him in the side a couple of times. A sound gurgled sound from the pit of his stomach. I stepped back with a disgusted look on my face, wrinkling my brow and lips. Officer Stanley's chest spazzed. His lifeless body regurgitated blood. Chunks of whoever he had eaten came bursting out of his mouth. The stench of it made me sick to my stomach. More and more of it bubbled out of his mouth. His lifeless body was animated, profusely regurgitating the wild amount of blood and flesh he'd consumed. The smell of it was indescribable.

I walked away from his putrid body, gagging. I heard another faint sound coming from one of the holding rooms. I gripped the handle of the door, it was locked. I didn't have the key to open it, so smashing my shoulder into the door seemed like a good idea. It wasn't. I tried the stallion way, taking a big step back and smashing my foot in the door. I blasted my already injured knee and cried out in pain. It hurt like a mother fucker. I took another step back and, as hard as I could, smashed my foot into the door. The door tipped off the hinges and smashed down onto the floor. I had a sudden gratitude that no criminals had ever thought to try that. The pain in my knee shot up and down my leg. Biting my lip, I pulled my gun up, ready to pop whoever it was.

I squinted and scanned the dimly lit cell. Officer McAllister! He was hiding in the corner of the room, curled up in the fetal position, waving his arm at me.

"Don't shoot!" he screamed frantically. "Don't shoot!" His head was tucked between both knees, his body quivering in fear. I walked over to him, aggressively grabbing his arm and pulling him to his feet.

"Get up, McAllister. Jesus." McAllister looked at me like he'd seen an angel.

"Man, am I glad to see you!" he said, quickly wrapping both arms around me in a massive bear hug. He squeezed me and cried at the same time.

I grabbed him with my right hand and barked, "Get the hell off me, pussy. What the hell is the matter with you?"

I pushed him into the wall, smacking him across the head. He stood there in shock.

"I'm sorry, Tommy. I'm just glad to see you, that's all." Without thinking, I slapped him across the face. With the most serious face I could muster, I said one word only: "No!" and pointed my finger in his face. "Don't!" He looked so young and bewildered. "Let's go!" I said as I grabbed his arm tightly and led him along behind me. a

As we exited the holding cell, I asked him, "What's going on? What the hell happened here?" He stood there quietly. "Erik!" He just stood there, looking at the floor. "Fuck, Erik!" I snapped my fingers at him.

He took a deep breath, "I don't know. I saw all this crazy shit on the news and rushed here for my shift and to find you. Then you left right away on the calls and pretty soon a bunch more crazy calls came in. It sounded like a stampede upstairs, but I just kept busy, like always. I should have gone upstairs to help." Tears rolled down his cheeks. "I was down here, filing away like a little pussy, and Officer Stanley came down with this crazy look in his eyes. His eyes were full of blood and half of his face was missing. His mouth dripped blood all over his body. Blood covered him. He was just like what I saw on the news. He screamed and hissed through his teeth. I saw a bunch of reporters get eaten alive on the TV. Fuck, I...I'm...I don't even know why I stayed down here. I knew something was wrong. When Stanley attacked me, he launched into the holding cell and the door slammed shut. I couldn't get out and he couldn't get in." McAllister took a deep breath. "I stood here, hoping that someone would come."

I placed my hand on Officer McAllister's shoulder and then touched his gun on his side, "Didn't they train you how to use this thing?" I shook my head in disappointment. "Let's go. We have to get out of here," I said, walking away from him. "The armory is down the hall. Go load up, while I check more of the rooms to see if there is anybody still alive."

Officer McAllister pulled his gun out of his holster, shaking like a scared child, walking to the armory. He loaded up on everything, filling a duffle bag full of shotguns, pistols, and semi automatic rifles. The rest of the cells were empty. I snatched the duffle bag from McAllister's hands, looking at him intensely, "You got my back right? Now's not the time to be such a pansy ass." I pointed at him, hoping my words would give the guy some kind of confidence. "Hey, be ready!" We walked down the hallway, turning to walk up the stairs. As we ascended, we heard chaos. Just as we got to the top of the stairs and we passed by the Chief's office, a group of twenty or so infected rushed through the doors of the police station. I stopped McAllister with my left arm, slowly walking backwards, trying not to make a sound. McAllister kicked that stupid ass bottle of scotch that Ronda had kicked out of the room when she was chasing me. It made a clunking sound. I thought to myself, 'Damn this fucking bottle, man!'

Everyone in freaking Denver, Colorado could hear the clink of that bottle hitting his shoe. We were trapped. The only way that wasn't blocked was back down the stairs. All of the infected rushed down the hallway at us, grabbing the collar of McAllister. I pulled him with me, jumping down the stairs, skipping steps, the weight of the bag of guns throwing me off balance. I fell to the floor. When I looked up, the infected were fighting their way through the two double doors, some of them falling down the stairs. McAllister grabbed my arm, helping me to my feet. One of the infected fell down the stairs, rolling past me, then quickly jumping to his feet and lunging at Erik.

I pulled my gun from my holster, shooting the infected man in the chest and again in the head. The flood rushed down the stairs, giving us only seconds to think. The infected came so fast that we had to sprint down the hallway and the pain still shot through my leg, slowing me down. The flood of infected rushed down the hallway, forcing us to resort to the stupidest idea ever. McAllister looked back at the flood of infected rushing down the hallway, the group of them clumsily tripping over one another, hissing and growling as they backed us into a literal corner. Both of us were freaked out and desperate, so I forced McAllister into a holding cell. I slammed the cell door shut behind us. One of the infected tried to bite at my hand as I slammed the door shut, but I pulled away too fast and she broke her front top teeth on the bar, snapping at me through the bars. Her mouth was profusely bleeding and angrily reached for me through the bars. More and more infected bodies smashed into the holding cells, the bars started to bend from the impact of the bodies. All the infected surrounded us and we were trapped in the cell. Hands and arms reached for us, attempting to grab Officer McAllister and I. We pressed our bodies against the wall away from the bars. We were sitting ducks. The bars were bowing. The only way out was through the small hole of a window. Neither of us would fit through that. More and more of the infected filled up the room, the group of them slammed their heads on the bars, hissing and growling; reaching at us, pulling the bars back and forth like wild animals. So many infected filled the room that it was impossible for any of them to move. The cell was completely surrounded. I was terrified out of my mind. I had to think quickly the cage wasn't going to hold much longer, not with that many bodies pushing at it. The bars were already old as crap and the cement that was holding in place was crumbling from the ground up.

I scanned the floor, looking at Officer McAllister, the bag of guns was gone. We didn't have the bag of guns. I must have dropped it by the stairs when I fell. This huge feeling of disappointment came over me.

"I dropped the guns by the stairs."

McAllister looked at me, shaking his head, "What the hell man? You're supposed to be this big, bad ass cop and you drop the guns? Come on, man!" Erik looked at me, sticking his middle finger in my face. I felt like punching him, but I'd screwed up big time. The only thing we had was the shotgun on my back and it only had about 6 shots and our pistols. There were 60 or more infected smashing their bodies against the steel bars. The bars squeaked and the cement chipped from the bottom to the,crumbling. It was just a matter of time until that cage was going to fall apart. I pulled my 9mm out, instead of shooting the infected, I pulled Officer McAllister away from the wall, cautiously and still out of reach of the infected. I fired a couple of shots at the cement surrounding the barred window, chipping away at it. With every second, those bars became less and less effective. I got a couple more shots off into the wall surrounding the window. We pulled at it as hard as we could, popping it loose.

"I'll go first because I know you're too weak to pull me out," I gave a smirk to Officer McAllister.

"Thanks. I'm glad you have a sense of humor while the world is ending all around us man," the replied.

"Sorry," I said, climbing my way out of the window, sliding across the ground to see if any of the infected were roaming around. It seemed clear. I reached to grab McAllister's arm just as the bars on the cage gave way, smashing down. The flood of infected smashed down, falling over one another. In a matter of seconds they had surrounded Erik, grabbing him, pulling him away from me. My grip on his arm started to give way. One of those assholes grabbed the side of his cheek, reaching its fingers into his mouth, pulling it back, separating the meat on his cheek from his skull. Another bit his arm, pulling out chunks as blood squirted everywhere. Officer McAllister screamed out. He had to have been in so much pain.

"HELP ME! TOMMY, HELP ME! DON'T LET ME DIE THIS WAY!" As we looked at each other, our eyes locked for a split second and then he disappeared into the bodies of the infected. Guilt washed over me. It should have been me. I didn't have time to wallow. Some of them lunged at me, throwing my body back, as they were fighting their way out of the window. I reached for my gun, shooting them in the face, and anywhere I could, stopping them from coming out. The sound of each gunshot put a target on me. Infected sprinted around the corner of the police station and from the surrounding alleys. I tried to haul ass down the alley, but my knee was busted so badly. Pain shot up to my hip, preventing me from running as fast as I could.

I had to get to the squad cars that were parked around the back. I smashed the window of the first car that I saw, throwing my body into the car and searching for the keys in the glove compartment. Infected threw themselves onto the car. The flood of them smashed into the car forcing it to lift off the ground. I revved up the engine and tried to get the car to move. An infected man came at me through the window. I turned and head butted him, stunning him enough to keep him back for a moment. The car moved forward, gaining speed and bowling over the infected that charged at it.

CHAPTER 7

The Cage Family

When it first started, I don't think anyone took it that seriously. I barely paid attention to the few reports surfacing on TV. One guy in Miami, reportedly strung out, began attacking his friend and was seen eating his face on a bridge. Eating some guy's face...that's a little much don't you think? I never did any drugs that made me want to eat one of my friend's faces. The news said it was a new drug (known as bath salts) and that he was so high that he ate his friend. Huh. I must have been getting old because in my day, we just did the wild weed. We'd never had crazy drugs that made you want to eat a guy's face. I continued to keep track of the local news as more and more reports kept coming in. Finally the government couldn't hide them any longer. The infection took over so fast, but no one paid attention... just like with every other disease. Swine flu took the globe- no one cared- everybody went on with their lives. Everyone I knew went on with no cares in the world. My friends and my neighbors just went on with their lives like nothing was happening. They all still kept going to their kids' soccer games and birthday parties. We even had a BBQ at my good friend Nathan's house. Little did we know that the infection would take the world in its hands and crush it.

Just like every morning, I got up, turned on the news, and made a good pot of coffee. No matter what, I made sure I had breakfast made for my two girls, Caroline and Lily. Lily was the youngest, about to turn 4. Caroline was the oldest. She was only 6, but acted like she was already old enough to move out and take on the world. It'd been really hard since their mother and I had decided to split up. I didn't even remember what half of our arguments were about. We just couldn't keep it together. I felt like nothing that I did was good enough and I could never make her happy. That's what hurt the most because all I'd ever wanted to do was make her happy. It was the same fight every damn day. Every time we fought, it would be about how unhappy she was. It killed me to be away from her! I wished I could tell her that I still loved her. Every time I saw her, I tried to bring myself to say it. I just wanted her back and I didn't care about the past. But then I would freeze. I don't know why because in my heart, I knew she loved me too and was too stubborn to say it. I didn't want to fight with her. I just wanted things to go back to the way they were. She picked the kids up for half the week and I had them for the rest and the weekends. It'd already been two years and my heart still beat hard and fast around her, like it had when I first saw her at work. We'd worked together for a couple of years and it's all an indie love story from there.

Caroline was the hardest to wake up. I'd have to yell at her all morning, "Get up, Caroline- it's time for school. I told you to go to bed earlier, now get up." Sometimes I would have to drag her out of bed, but somehow she would always find a way to fall back asleep anywhere she was. I'd found her asleep in her laundry basket and in the bathtub (when she was supposed to be brushing her teeth). Lily was easier. I'd tell her to get up and in her little voice she'd always respond, "Ok daddy". She'd be up and ready to go. It wasn't easy being a single dad. Everyday I learned new things about my girls, and I never had all the answers, but I wouldn't have traded it for anything in the world.

All of us were flying out to Los Angeles to see my parents for the weekend. For some reason that cup of coffee was the best I'd had in a long time. I sat there, sipping it, staring out the window; watching the leaves of the tree blowing in the wind. The sun beamed through the tree, onto my face, and I could feel the warmth. In that moment, I felt like I was right where I needed to be. I could hear the sound of the news in the background. But then, that beeping sound that the news does when it's on standby suddenly caught my attention. I walked over to the TV, sipping my coffee gently, the girls giggled in the background. Just as I reached over to grab the remote, someone pounded at the door. It startled me, making me spill my coffee all over the front of my shirt.

"Damn it! One second!". I tried to clean my shirt, but the pounding on the door became more violent. "Hold on one second!" I walked over to the door and I noticed that it was Anabelle. She was frantically pounding at the door. Confused, I opened the door. Anabelle came rushing in, her hands and face were covered in blood. I was really confused as she ran down the hallway to the bathroom. Tears were falling down her face.

"What the hell happened?" I asked her. I didn't get an answer from her. The girls saw her and fear washed over them. Their mother was covered in blood. Walking behind her, I repeatedly asked her, "What the hell is going on?!" Finally, I grabbed her arm and I pulled her back to me. She broke down, falling to her knees. The girls stared at her, terrified.

"Go in your rooms girls. I need to talk to your mom." She stood there on her knees, weeping and shaking. I tried to calm her down. I softly asked her again, "Anabelle what's going on? Calm down and tell me what's going on..."

Lifting her head from my chest, which was now covered in blood, she looked at me as I brushed away the hair that was clinging to the blood and tears on her face. "I don't know what happened! I woke up this morning and my dad was eating my mom! Then he attacked me. It was like he was trying to kill me too..." Anabelle sat there, continuing to shake, crying hysterically. "He was chasing me around the house screaming and hissing. I didn't know what to do so I grabbed my keys from the coffee table and ran out of the door.

He chased me and jumped on top of me and he was hitting me and punching me in the face! Then he was throwing up blood. I grabbed one of the potted plants and I hit him in the head. I was able to get away and get in my car, but he jumped at the car, punching it and he chased me a block or so. After I took off, I didn't know what to do or where to go, so I came here."

I sat there in shock, listening to the story she'd just told me. Then she told me that the neighborhood was going crazy. People were chasing people, cars were running people over; it was a war zone. She saw another man shoot a guy in the head. I couldn't believe what I was hearing. We both stood there in the bathroom. It was like something out of a soap opera. I didn't know what to feel: confusion, shock...what?...I couldn't pinpoint it. What the hell was going on? I didn't know what to do. I felt like we would be safer at my parent's lake house until this blew over. I told Anabelle to come with us. It would be safer to be with us than to stay here by herself. Suddenly, it was dead quiet. We both stood there looking into each other's eyes. From the corner of my eye, I saw a shadow in my bedroom window. One of the infected came smashing through the window... then more, one right after the other. They started smashing through all of the bedroom windows. I pushed Anabelle out of the way and I grabbed the door knob, slamming the door shut, attempting to lock them in the bedroom. The infected slammed their bodies into the door harder and harder. The girls were standing behind us, screaming at the top of their lungs. The sound of their screams echoed through the house. More and more of the infected began attacking the window; breaking their way into each room.

"We have to go!" I told Anabelle. Each of us grabbed a girl. Their screams continued to echo through the house as one infected crashed through the girls' bedroom, jumped over the bed, ran into the door; hissing and snarling at Anabelle while she was holding Lily Feeling the need to protect them, I ran back down the hallway and I smashed my shoulder into its chest before it could grab them. In a panic, both of us held the girls, and as more and more of them flooded into the house chasing us down the hallway, I yelled, "Get to the car! Take the girls and get to the car!"

Handing Caroline to Anabelle, I began to fight them off to give my family time to get to the car in the garage. Anabelle and the girls frantically ran through the kitchen to the garage door. With my back turned, one of the infected jumped on me, tackling me to the ground. I had to think quickly if there was going to be any way that my family and I were going to get out alive. As the infected and I struggled, we crashed to the floor. I landed on my side, but I noticed that the fire poker was there. I reached for it before the other infected came rushing down the hallway. I tried everything I could to get away. When I jumped to my feet, the infected chased me past the living room, into the kitchen. One of them lunged at me; I shoved the poker through its mouth, plunging it into the back of the throat, piercing through the back of the neck. I jumped from the door of the kitchen onto the car and two or three infected leapt after me, falling off the hood of the car. Anabelle was in the driver's seat throwing the car in to reverse and speeding through the garage door. Hanging onto the hood as hard as I could, the garage door smashed on top of me. The car backed out of the driveway with the infected chasing us. I could feel the bodies of the infected jumping on top of the garage door, which was still on top of me, and the car.

Anabelle sped from the driveway without looking and another car speeding down the road smashed the back end of our car, spinning it out of control tossing me, the garage door, and two of the infected flew off of the car-landing on the lawn in front of the house. I felt every bone in my body crack. My head slammed onto the ground and my vision became blurry from the impact. The infected jumped on the car that hit us. A woman in the front seat began screaming at the top of her lungs in complete panic while one of the infected slammed his head continuously into the windshield of her car until it shattered. Another one threw its body into the passenger side of the car. The woman's blood curdling screams caught every infected person's attention. Tearing into the car, one of them grabbed her hair and bit the side of her cheek pulling the skin and meat from the bone. Another one grabbed her arm, biting chunks of flesh. The sound of her screams quickly turned into a whimper. I forced myself to get up, the pain shooting through my entire body, crippling me. The girls began screaming, their mom unconscious in the front seat, as they sat there watching this woman get torn to pieces from the blood hungry infected. As I opened the door, I pushed Anabelle over to the passenger seat; the girls' frantic screams caught the attention of the infected. They began attacking our car. While I backed away from the accident, one of them remained on the hood of the car. Once I got a good distance from the other car, I spun in a complete 180...tires screeching and peeling out. The infected man flew from the hood of the car into the fire hydrant on the corner breaking its back. I desperately tried to calm the girls down, while speeding away. It was hard to concentrate on driving the car. The infected chased the car until they were unable to keep up with it. I flew down the road. Anabelle was still unconscious in the passenger seat; her body and head bouncing around as we sped through the chaos that had become our city. People were chasing other people around like savage animals; eating one another. A big jet airliner came falling from the sky. I could feel the vibration of it as it screamed past the car, crashing. The wing of the jet scraped the ground leaving a trail of asphalt chunks. The airliner turned to its right side ripping into pieces as it demolished houses. Big explosions lit up the neighborhood like a small atomic bomb going off. The car swerved out of control from the impact of the plane crash. I had no choice but to smash my foot on the brake, slowing the car down to regain control, and find a way out of the city. Infected from all over were chasing the car; a few turned into fifty and all of them were running as fast as they could to catch up to the car. Caroline and Lily had no idea what was going on. Lily sat next to her sister holding her as tightly as she could. Caroline screamed at the top of her lungs. I didn't know what to do or where to go. All I knew was that I needed to get out of the city as fast as I could! I needed to protect my family... any way possible. A flood of them rushed on the left forcing us to turn into the city. Taking a hard right, one car sped past me, thinking they could blow past the infected. In my rearview mirror, I saw that the other car was already consumed by the infected... they'd stopped the car dead in its tracks and the bodies had overwhelmed it like river water, drowning it. The bodies of the infected forced us to get on the on ramp to the city.

CHAPTER 8

The City

Quickly the roads became packed. Cars flooded the streets, the people were running everywhere. The infected consumed everything...even the bridge...Fuck! I had to stop the car. There was nowhere to go. The pack of cars prevented us from going anywhere as the flood of the infected took over the onramp to the bridge. People were sitting in their cars, trying to get away...stuck there like sitting ducks: a feast for every infected body. Men and women carrying their families were lost; not knowing what to do. The faces... some of the people looked like they didn't even know what was going on. They had no idea that the infection had spread through the city. In my mirror, I could see the devastation of the infected as they took each person who sat in their cars. Anabelle was still unconscious in the passenger seat. The girls were unaware that the flood of infected, consuming everything in their way, was only 30 feet behind us. I screamed at the top of my lungs, trying to wake Anabelle up. I had no choice but to slap her to wake her up.

"Daddy, what's happening?" Caroline's little voice came from the back seat. "Lets go girls. We have to go. Get your seat belts off. We have to go sweetheart." I kept repeating myself. I began to panic; the seat belt was stuck. I couldn't get it off, their mom was still unconscious and the flood of the infected was closing in. My hands shook violently. Out the back window more and more of them approached. I noticed a little girl standing next to a car crying and yelling for her mom, her parents nowhere in sight. Scared people ran past her, running each other over, pushing and shoving each other in fear. Mothers carried their babies and children ran for their lives. Finally, I popped the seat belt out and pulled the girls out of the car. Anabelle was still unconscious in the passenger seat. I did everything that I could to wake her up, but I ran out of time. I had to make a choice: her or the kids. I had seconds to make that choice. All of us die together, or leave Anabelle behind to save the girls. I picked up Lily and grabbed the hand of Caroline.

I ordered, "Hold my belt and whatever you do, don't let go!" They were only a couple of feet behind us now. The little girl holding her bear by the car cried, desperately trying to understand the panic of every person running by her. Picking up both of my little girls, I ran as fast as I could, past the people still sitting in their cars. I tried not to look back. I gave it everything I had. I pushed forward. I had to get the girls as far away as I could. I wasn't strong enough to carry both girls in my arms, my arms began to give up. My lungs were unable to get enough air; my asthma was kicking in. There was a bus two cars ahead of us. I had no choice but to try to hide from the infected. I felt a hand on my back pushing me and the girls into the back of a truck, slamming my body into the tailgate. I looked back. I could still see our car, and Anabelle getting pulled out of the car as hoards of infected bit her unconscious body. I choked back a sob. One jumped on top of her and her body disappeared behind the cars. We had to go. I had to let go.

I regained my grip on Caroline and Lily and ran to the door of the bus, putting both of the girls down, trying to push the door on the bus in; it was stuck. I slammed my shoulder into the door repeatedly. I looked back as one of the infected, standing behind the bus, stared us down. He walked slowly to us, knowing there was nowhere for us to go. Boom! A gunshot rang off, startling me and the girls. Both of them grabbed at my legs. The side of the infected man's head painted the side of the bus; blood sprayed all over the side of the bus. I looked to my left and I saw an old man standing there. He was getting out of the passenger side of a car, revolver in his hand, the barrel still smoking. A handful of infected attacked him and gunshots popped off in the air as he struggled. One of them jumped on his back taking a chunk of his neck out. The old man pulled up the revolver, putting it to the forehead of the infected as it pulled the meat from his neck. BOOM! This guy was like Clint Eastwood. One of them latched onto his arm. He looked at me and gave me a look that I immediately understood. He threw me the gun. I stood there in amazement while the old guy screamed at the top of his lungs. To take attention away from us, he pushed off his attacker and began running, waving his arms wildly and screaming. Most of them chased him down and he waited for most of them to get close, standing by the rail of the bridge. As they lunged at him, biting him more and more, the mass shoved him over the edge of the bridge. Dozens of the infected jumped over the bridge after him. They plummeted to the ground; bodies falling everywhere! One right after the other smashed onto the pavement, creating a soup bowl of infected bodies; giving me and the girls enough time to get into the bus. Smashing my shoulder against the door of the bus once again, I finally busted it open. Grabbing both girls, I pushed them onto the bus. More and more of the infected surrounded us. One of them grabbed my foot as I was climbing on the bus, tripping me on the stairs and causing me to drop the gun. It slid to the middle of the bus and the girls began screaming in fear. The first thought that popped into my head was to kick it on the face as hard as I could. Using all of the power I had left for each blowing kick to the right side of its jaw, I forced its neck to twist. It continued to claw and scratch at my legs and I kicked it in the jaw one more time. As it briefly released me, I began frantically climbing my way up the stairs, kicking the door shut. The infected girl pushed herself off of the car and lunged at the door. Slamming her into the door over and over was my only defense. It shattered the bottom glass of the door. She reached for me, the door began to give way...I had to hold the door with my foot, but more and more bodies of the infected gathered around the door. The weight of them made it harder for me to hold the door.

I screamed at Caroline, "Grab daddy the gun sweetheart. I need you to grab daddy the gun!". She stood there in the middle of the bus, hysterical, scared out her mind, frozen... unable to move. The door of the bus was giving way. I wasn't sure that I could hold it . More of the infected forced their way against the door snarling and hissing. The infected girl's arms reached for my legs through the shattered door of the bus.

Looking over to Caroline, I screamed at her at the top of my lungs, forcing her to give me her attention. "Caroline! I need you to give daddy the gun. Please Caroline I need the gun...damn it!" She still stood there frozen. Both my legs were ready to give at any second...letting the crowd of infected in would make me the first meal and I knew I wouldn't be able to protect the girls in the position I was in. Lily reached over, grabbed the gun and slid it to me, but it only slid a couple of inches. Caroline stood there frozen, sobbing. Lily had to reach over and slide the gun to me one more time, putting it inches away from my reach.

"I need the gun sweetheart..." Neither of them would go any further. I had to let the door go if I was going to be able to grab the gun. I had to make a choice; a choice that could decide the fate of my daughters. Reaching for the gun I let go of the door, letting the group of infected into the bus. I had seconds to react, grabbing the gun, popping one of them in the head while the others shoved their way into the bus. Another gunshot hit one in the shoulder. Running to the back of the bus grabbing Caroline and Lily, I pushed them to the back of the bus. The infected pushed their way down the aisle of the bus. One of them looked at me, blood dripping from his mouth, his eyes connecting with mine. His blood infused eyes put a crazy amount of fear through my entire body. There were only two shots left and ten or so infected forcing their way through the bus. The girls screamed. I had no ideas. We were trapped... there was nowhere to go. The infected rushed down the aisle, charging at us.

I didn't want my two girls to live through the infection eating the flesh from their bones and having to suffer the slow and agonizing death of being consumed alive. Two shots. With a gut wrenching sob, I shot my Lily and then Caroline. The infected rushed me... ten or more bodies jumped on me. I could feel the teeth of each one sink into my skin. One of them bit into my neck, pulling the muscle along with it and then one of them bit my ear off. I felt every second of the pain. They continued to rip my other ear from the side of my head. More of the infected were on top of me; the weight of them buckling my knees. Their cold fingers shoved into my stomach and pulled my insides out. I began dying slowly, watching them eat me from the inside out.

CHAPTER 9

Pastor Vince Bernal

Every Sunday before church I got down on my knees and prayed for a good hour. I prayed that God would give me the strength to give his word, give me the power to reach people that couldn't be reached. Times had changed; things in the world seemed more complicated. Evil had filled the streets. In my personal belief, the end of the world was right around the corner. It was time to prepare for the day that Hell on earth would break out upon us. I tried to save as many souls as I could, even mine, but each day, every hour, was a struggle.

Every Sunday our typical group came. Sometimes, I wished I could get to more people; new people to spread the word. Randy and Evelyn were our biggest leaders. Lord, I wished I didn't know everybody's business, but new travels fast in the church. It seemed that everyone but Evelyn knew that Randy was having an affair with one of the girls he worked with. It was a shame. I really liked Evelyn. I'd tried to have a talk with Randy, but every time I came close to bringing it up, I'd cower and change the subject. Last Sunday after church he'd come up to me with this look of guilt, like something was wrong, and it was eating away at him. Twirling his fingers back and forth, he'd said he needed to talk to me, that he had something huge to get off his chest. I finally thought that he was going to talk about it, but he'd quickly panicked when Evelyn walked in the chapel asking if he was ready to go. Then he'd just smiled, put his hand on my shoulder and said, "Maybe some other time." I'd told him sure, and that I pray for them a lot. Time would tell, I guess, on that one.

Tommy Maestas and his wife Jenny would come every Sunday too. They had a son named Carson. He was a really cute kid. They'd always seemed so happy; a beautiful family. Tommy even used to come to play poker with a couple of the guys in the church. I'd even step in sometimes…ok, I was there every time. But I hadn't seen Officer Tommy that much since Jenny and Carson were killed in the accident. Once in a while Tommy would come in and sit in the back and stay for a couple of minutes and leave. That was honestly one of the saddest funerals I had ever done. It tore him apart, as it would anybody, losing their entire family.

Mrs.Miller was loyal too. She was an elderly woman in her eighties. Her husband, Edgar, had passed about a year before. Every Sunday, even on the first Wednesday of the month, she wore the same white dress and shoes; the same hat. Mrs. Miller would always say it wasn't proper for a lady to come to church like the girls did 'nowadays' in their street clothes. She always had a chip on her shoulder like she was high class, but she'd lived in an apartment down the street and she would take the bus every Sunday to church. I don't think I ever saw her in a different dress. She always sat in the front row and prayed that one day she would be reunited with Edgar. Edgar was one of our good poker friends, too. He'd said he always had to get away from Mrs. Miller before "the old bag gave him a heart attack". I know what you're thinking, a pastor that gambles, for shame. I did it with my money and then I'd put the winnings into the offering for the church. I know it's still bad to gamble, but everyone has their demons. I don't consider myself better than anybody. I am a man, but just because I am a man of the cloth, doesn't mean that I'm perfect.

Clara was the lady in the tight red dresses. She was beautiful and boy, did she have a body that could kill! Legs for days. Clara never wore a different kind of lipstick; always red. Lady in Red. That was her name around the church. That, or slut. I remember hearing some of the wives say she was always trying to go after everyone's husbands but her own. She pretended like she was innocent around the women in the church. She would attend every church bake sale and fundraiser and pretend to get along with all the women, but all of them knew what she was trying to do. The wives would get bent out of shape each time they caught their husbands staring at her. Most of them would watch their husbands like hawks. She finally got caught cheating on her husband, Bill, with the garden boy. He'd caught them in the bed that they both slept in. I didn't know why she still came to church. She acted like nothing had ever happened. They went through a divorce. Bill still came as well and they would sit on opposite sides of the church. Poor Bill stared at her the whole time. I don't even think he blinked. I think he came to church to watch her every move.

I could go on with everyone's details and stories for hours. Lord, I wished I didn't know so much. I did try to stay out of it as much as I could. Being a man of God, I didn't want to get caught up in all the gossip and bad things that happened in my flock, but I wanted to do the best I could to help those around me.

I'd never been married. I went to a Catholic school for most of my young years. I'd always wanted to get married, I just never could find that one person that would love me and take all the responsibilities of being a reverend's wife. I knew it wasn't easy, but I just wanted someone I could give my love to. Clara has always made her passes at me, but being a man of God, I had to respectfully decline every time. Don't get me wrong, it crossed my mind a couple of times. She was so beautiful and it'd been a long time for me. It wasn't like girls were coming to my house to break down my door to be with me. I was getting up to my 40's, I didn't have kids, and I wasn't getting married any time in the near future. I wondered if it was God's plan for me to die pathetically and utterly alone.

A lot of the people in the church kept asking me if the infection was the end of the world. The news was going crazy with the sadness of the rampant infection. I didn't think it was any different than swine flu and any other disease that came and went. The only thing I could tell them was that if it was, we needed to get ready and be prepared for the day. The news broadcasts really scared everyone. Each Sunday that passed had less and less people show up to church. Some wouldn't even leave their houses. A couple had already decided to kill themselves by shooting themselves and burning their house down; taking everything they owned with them. When I heard that, I for sure knew that things were only going to get worse. The first Wednesday of the month, we would have an evening service. No one ever came anymore. Sometimes I would think to myself, "why do I even bother?", but faith kept me going.

That night, though, it was unusually packed for a typical Wednesday evening service. I knew things were going crazy out in the world, but I was kind of excited to see that many people sitting in my church! I guess my prayers were really answered. Every face in each row had the look on their face that they were terrified. Families I didn't even know had shown up. I could read it on every face that came through that door. Parents were holding their children tightly, in fear, and couples were holding each other tightly. I guess they were all there hoping that going to church would save their lives one way, or another. The church was quiet; you could have heard a pin drop, coughs echoed. Every single eye was on me like I was going to be the one delivering the words that would save the world. I had always thought that I would be ready for such a moment, but as I stood there, my knees locked and my hands were sweaty. My cleric's uniform had a pool of sweat drowning my body. Before I could even get a word out, Bill stood up in the back of the church coughing and holding his stomach. His eyes were filling with blood and then he began throwing up blood all over Mrs.Miller, covering her white dress. Bill grabbed her hat, pulling it off, as he fell to the ground. Mrs.Miller's jaw dropped in shock. Bill began screaming in pain; the entire church blew up in a panic. No one moved, paralyzed by the fear of what was going to happen next. Bill fell over on Mrs.Miller and in that split second, he went from being Bill, to this infected monster. His arms began swinging as he began hissing and snarling. He laid on top of Mrs.Miller. She was stuck under Bill, screaming for someone to help her. No one even moved. I could hear her elderly scream. The weight of Bill's body crushed her, as the pew fell back, blocking the doorway. Everyone stood there, frozen, watching Bill attack this elderly woman. Bill grabbed her head, slamming it into the ground. Her frail arms quickly became limp; her body lifeless in front of the door. Bill jumped to his feet, blocking anyone from running out of the church, all the while staring at every one crowded in each of the pews. He was like a bull, hissing and snarling, ready to charge anyone who came close to him. Mrs.Miller unexpectedly rolled over and began throwing up blood profusely. Her eyes became blood infused, in that split second, and she leapt to her feet like she was 20 years old. Both of them stood in front of the door. Both of them lunged at the crowd, swinging their arms, clawing at anyone they could get to. Mrs.Miller flung her 95 pound body onto Clara, pulling her hair, biting her on the neck, and then jumped to the next person. Everyone in the church rushed to the door, but Bill jumped ferociously, clawing whomever he could get ahold of. Clara fell to her knees, holding her stomach with one hand, while the other tried to stop the blood from gushing out of her neck. The church roared in panic. People began trampling over each other, pushing each other over. The infected from the outside of the church began rushing in the front door like a group of moths to a flame, creating a horrendous entanglement of panicked folks and hungry infected.

 Clara snapped her head up: hissing, attacking the first person in her sight. She tackled the gentleman next to her, biting his face, pulling the cheek from the bone. That poor man screamed in pain while her fist balled up and pounded his body into a pulp. She bounced his head off the floor and then lunged for his neck, pulling a chunk out. The man began choking on his own blood. One person right after the other dropped. In mere seconds, they became infected and attacked one another. My church had become a bloodbath. And my flock...my Lord! The once white rug turned red from the pool of blood soaking it. People began slipping and falling all over the church while the infected attacked anything that moved. It was like shooting fish in a barrel. The beautiful wood stained pews covered were in blood. Bill tackled Henry, another group leader, into the pew. I stood at the altar, watching the whole thing...watching the bloodbath ensue...I couldn't move. The infected rushed in through the front door, rushed into the crowd of people trying to get out. They were so desperate...any way possible... pushing one another, trampling their way out, as the infected fought their way in. The screams of everyone echoed in the hall of the church like a chorus. I remained frozen. Clara was chewing someone's intestines. It was like something out of a bad horror film. The guy just laid there, screaming, or rather, attempting to scream as he choked on his own blood and tried to put his own intestines back in. I couldn't believe what I was seeing. This wasn't the way things were supposed to happen. God! People should have been given the right to be raptured if this was the end. Why were we all still there to witness Hell on earth? The church was supposed to be a peaceful place, a sanctuary for God's people. My body was frozen, my knees were locked. I couldn't move. My mind was telling me to get out, but the fear and utter disbelief consumed me, preventing me from even breathing. As I stood at the altar, I slowly grabbed my bible. I had no choice. I tried to gain any type of courage and run to hide behind the enormous Jesus statue which stood behind me. I was a coward. I didn't have the strength to even help anyone. I stood there watching this massacre unfold right in front of my eyes and hid behind the Jesus statue. As I peaked my head out to see what was going on, Clara was standing there, her fist clenched into a ball; blood dripping, staining the floors. Her once lovely red dress was painted with the blood of every victim she had consumed. It was like she knew I was there the whole time. I fell back and began crying; scared to death. I couldn't even get the words out. Clara stood there, knowing she had her victim right where she wanted. Crawling and sliding my pathetic body back, I held my arms up in defense; like it was going to stop her from lunging at me and sinking her teeth into me. She stood there hissing, clenching her teeth, grinding them back and forth. She had so much anger! She was completely unaware as her teeth began cracking and shattering. The blood of her victims dripped from her mouth. I was terrified. I kept willing myself to get up and just run. My mind was saying it, but my body wasn't doing it. Clara leapt for me, pouncing on top of me, her knee jamming into my ribs taking my breath. My arms were still up in defense, but her tiny fists pounded my face. For such a small person, her fists felt like Thor's hammer, smashing my face and my head, crushing it into the ground. I could feel her teeth sink into my hand pulling the meat from the bottom of my palm. I began screaming and it seemed the louder I screamed, the harder and more vicious she got. Clara spit out the chunk of my hand and when I looked at her, even just for that split second, deep down I knew that was the end. Your life does flash in front of your eyes. I wasn't going to be taken in the rapture, or die peacefully. Bill rushed up to the altar, and bit into my thigh. I began kicking; doing everything I could to stop him from sinking his teeth in again. I tried to prevent the painful slow death as best as I could, but more and more infected joined in, jumping on top of me; eating at me like I was a Vegas buffet. I could feel their fingertips piercing my skin. Clara lunged for my neck, sinking her teeth into my throat, piercing my jugular. The air from my lungs escaped through my throat. Blood bubbled up from the air trying to escape and gushed down my throat with each painful inhalation. I felt my heart beat faster and faster, pumping the warm blood into my mouth and my lungs. With each beating pulse from my heart, more and more of my own blood drowned me. No more air. I believe at that point the pain was so overwhelming, the shock began taking over. I could feel the grip of a hand on my lung as it was being pulled from under my rib cage, detaching from my body. My body convulsed. No white light; only darkness. All I could see was darkness. I could feel myself fade away slowly into it. My brain began filling with electric memories of my life. They fired off in my head like files being deleted. Everything I knew began to disappear. Everything that made me human was gone. I knew nothing but anger and aggression. I wanted to destroy anything in my way.

CHAPTER 10

Channel 4 news

"Thank you for joining us. I'm Ben O'Malley. If you're just tuning in, we have just been informed of breaking news. Martial Law is now in effect. For those of you that don't know, Martial Law is: the law temporarily imposed upon an area by state or national military forces when civil authority has broken down. 2.The law administered by military forces that is invoked by the government in an emergency when the civilian law enforcement agencies are unable to maintain public order or safety. By enforcing this, the government has asked that you please stay in your homes and lock all your doors. We suggest you board up any windows and/or entrances that may have easy access. Please, do not come out of your houses for any reason. Stock up on water and supplies as soon as you can. I have been notified that martial law will be in effect immediately. Again, I say, this martial law will be in effect immediately. If you don't need to leave your home, we insist that you stay there. Military personnel will be evacuating by district, so please be patient and do not attempt to evacuate yourselves. Ok folks, I have just been notified that we are now going to be joined by Dr. Malcolm Heater from the CDC to learn more about this virus. Thank you for joining us, Dr. Heater. What can you tell us about the current state of affairs?"

"Well, Bill, from what we have discovered through a series of tests, is that this virus is as powerful as it can get. I've been doing this for many years. I have never seen anything like it. I don't want to alarm anyone, but if you do come in contact with the virus it is very important that you quarantine yourself, or the individual, immediately. I understand this is a difficult thing to hear, but for the safety of everyone around you, it is very important that you quarantine yourself. I can reassure you that this is no joking matter. This virus is lethal and it can't be stopped at this point. It moves at such a rapid pace. I do assure you all that we are doing everything we can to find a cure at this time. The virus is moving at such an outstanding pace it's only a matter of time before……before…" Dr. Heater paused from the frog settling in on his throat and took a deep breath, pulling his glasses off his face and cleaning them in a nervous sweat.

Ben looked very worried, his face penetrating and firm, looking deep in the camera. "How much time do you suppose we have Dr. Heater?", Ben asked nervously.

The doctor placed his glasses back on to his face, sweat dripping, "In the matter of time that this virus is spreading…I…"

Ben cut him off before Dr. Heater could finish his sentence, "How much time do we have Dr. Heater?!"

"Well…hours, Mr. O'Malley, hours."

Nervous sighs echoed throughout the studio.

Dr. Heater continued, anxiously, "It's just a matter of time until it hits every major city and rural neighborhood. So like I said before, a cure has yet to be discovered, but I will tell you this: my team and I have been working relentlessly! Countless hours! And we will not stop until we find a cure for this virus.".

Ben again stared deeply into the camera, wiping the sweat from his lip, "Dr. Heater what can you tell us about the symptoms of this virus?"

"The virus consumes its victims in a matter of seconds. The symptoms are severe aggression and anger, blood draining from the eyes, the pupils dilate. The intentions of the infected are to kill anything and everything in their path. If anyone is showing flu-like symptoms, please be aware that they might be infected. The flu-like symptoms last for a matter of a couple hours. This disease is powerful and it takes a matter of seconds, once the flu type symptoms begin to pass, for it to consume its victims. Please be careful and God bless."

"There you have it folks: Some powerful and terrifying words. Thank you Dr. Heater. Dr. Heater has been working for the CDC for over 15 years. Let's pray to God that a cure can quickly be discovered as we have just learned that China, India, and Russia have all fallen. All middle eastern countries with troop support are actively deployed to assist with national military personnel in evacuation. All of the United Kingdom is in disarray and we do not know if the entire area has fallen prey to this vicious disease. We will keep you informed with further details, but we are now going to go to Mia Sandoval in downtown Los Angeles. Mia can you tell us what is going on? What's the latest news from down there?".

"Thank you, BIll. It appears that the infection has spread rapidly throughout the streets of downtown Los Angeles... it seems in a matter of minutes. The people that are, in fact, infected are running rampant hunting everyone in sight. Those that remain infection free are failing to follow martial law and are in the streets rioting and looting. I've never seen anything like this. Just a few minutes ago we were forced to run for our very lives. Police and Military have lost containment. Michael and I witnessed a gentleman pull an elderly woman out of her car and beat her to death in a matter of seconds. She then became infected within the minute. I can't even describe it, Bill; the agility that this elderly woman had was unreal!She began chasing my cameraman, Michael, and myself. We were forced to run and find immediate shelter in this convenience store, where police officers have barricaded us in. It seems the Infected are doing everything they can to get in! Police officers have been forced to open fire at any infected that have made their way in. Nothing seems to stop them. They are using their heads and bodies to smash the glass and bars surrounding the store. Oh...Oh my God. It seems we...we have a situation! The infected have made their way into the store."

Michael threw his camera down, "I'm done. They don't pay me enough for this shit." He ran for the back door.

Mia cried out, "They are here! This is it! Run Michael!". Mia screamed in a panic as the infected made their way in. Two police officers began firing into the sea of infected that surged their way into the store. Shots echoed throughout the store. One of the infected lunged for one of the officers, sinking his teeth into the officer's neck, shredding it as blood sprayed violently. Rapidly shooting anything, firing his gun into the air, the police officer was tackled and thrown into a shelf. The other police officer shot the infected in the back of the head, popping off the back of its skull. He continued, also firing at anything that moved in front of him. More and more of the infected rushed into the convenience store, trampling over one another. Mia and Michael found their way into the back of the convenience store. Michael stood there, thinking, his mind racing a million miles a second while his heart pumped through his chest. Michael noticed the green glowing exit sign. Grabbing Mia's arm aggressively, he dragged her to the back exit door. Mia's shrill screams captured the attention of all the infected that had ambushed the front of the store. The one police officer was consumed by the pile of bodies jumping on him, one right after the other. The camera, still rolling, was kicked into the wall. As it spun, all those still capable of watching heard the police officer screaming at the top of his lungs, witnessing more infected flood the store and rip him from limb to limb. The flood of bodies followed the screaming to the back of the store. Michael and Mia slammed their bodies into the door, swinging it wide open, only to be met by yet another herd of infected awaiting them in the back. Michael and Mia tripped over one another, falling into the middle of the crowd of infected. Instantly, the crowd of infected from inside, burst out and meshed into those already poised outside. The hoards landed on top of Mia and Michael, and they began clawing and scratching at both of them. Mia shrieked at the top of her lungs for someone to help them, but not a soul was in sight. The microphones rustled; clouding the sound for a second. The infected pulled the microphones that were attached to them. Every sound of the infected snarling and hissing, the blood curdling screams of Mia and Michael...all of it echoed through the microphones. The nation heard every grueling sound of their slow and painful deaths; every moment of them getting pulled slowly apart from the inside out, unable to escape.

Ben O'Malley sat there in utter and complete shock, holding his ear piece into his ear, his mouth dropped open, as he listened to Mia and Michael's agonizing deaths on live TV. Everyone in the studio was quiet. Everyone was paralyzed, in shock. The sound editor was so frozen in fear that he couldn't cut the horrific sound. In the background of the studio a voice echoed to cut the sound. Ben O'Malley sat at the anchor desk, not making a sound, not even moving a muscle. His left hand reached over to his tie loosening it. The sound of Mia and Michaels screams changed from blood curdling, to a labored gurgling.

Ben finally brought himself back and barked, "Cut the damn sound! Cut the sound!" Frustrated, he slammed his hand on the desk. The studio was dead quiet. You could almost hear the heartbeats of everyone there. Ben reached to his ear.

"I apologize folks. What you just heard was deeply disturbing and I truly am sorry that you had to hear that. I have just been notified that the president of the United States, Alex Griego, has been killed, along with Vice President, Jonathan Davis. It is not clear what has happened to both of them, but again, both the President and Vice President have been killed. I am now being told that we are going off the air. We tried to stay on as long as we could to keep feeding the news to you, but we will be switching over the national Stand By screen. Dear God help us. Please folks, whatever you do, please stay in your homes until military personnel can evacuate you. So much has been lost...do whatever you can to be safe. This will be my last broadcast with channel 4 news and it has been my pleasure to serve the city of Los Angeles for 26 years. I will be praying for every one of you. Please stay safe and goodbye."

Ben wiped his mouth with his hand and slowly stood up. His other hand held his tie, his head shaking as he hung it and ripped the microphone from his body throwing it to the back of the studio in pure frustration and fear. The broadcast was still rolling when Ben, with a shaky, quivering voice broke down into tears, "I have to get home to my family. I need to find my wife and kids." Suddenly, the broadcast cut out as it switched over to the national stand by screen. Ben placed his hands on the back of his anchor chair and looked straight at the floor. A big crashing sound came from the big double doors that led into the newsroom, catching the attention of everyone who had been lost in thought and shock. Complete silence stifled the room as everyone stared at the double doors; again a gut wrenching crash from the doors. Ben looked at Steve, his longtime cameraman, and barely croaked, "They're here." Both doors slammed open and a flood of infected rushed in the newsroom. One of the infected lunged at Steve, biting his ear off, as he tackled him to the ground. Everyone in the news studio erupted in a panic. Another infected jumped on the anchor stage, rushing at Ben. With quick instinct, Ben shoved the chair into the gut of the infected pushing him off the anchor stage just as more of them barreled through the double doors heading directly at Ben. Again quickly reacting, Ben climbed the ladder that led up to the light beam. One of the infected bloody hands grabbed at Ben's shoe, covering it in blood. Ben panicked and almost fell down into the crowd of infected. Dozens of them pulled at his legs. It took every ounce of his strength as he held on for dear life to be able to finally escape the grasp of the infected. Shakily, Ben tried to climb up the ladder, but his blood smattered shoe forced him to slip and lose his grip completely on the ladder. He fell a good 10 feet, through a gap of the infected, before his leg caught him, hammering his entire upper body into the ground, breaking his neck. His lifeless body hung from the ladder while the infected began forcing their already blood covered hands into the warm torso of Ben, pulling his intestines and his bladder, eating at him violently. The screams of every poor soul that remained in that newsroom rang out sorrowfully as the bloodbath unfolded in quicktime. One by one, the living awaited the inevitability of death. The bright lights of the studio cut out to the red emergency lights, spinning, making it impossible for anyone to escape. It was so dark. The infected ambushed anyone trying to get out. One by one, each scream became silent...not one soul had a chance to make it out alive.

www.ingramcontent.com/pod-product-compliance
Lightning Source LLC
LaVergne TN
LVHW011710060526
838200LV00051B/2832